EXIT THE DRAGON

HEIDE GOODY

IAIN GRANT

1

EXIT THE DRAGON

Maegor spotted the man moving chairs in the long hall and initially took him for a member of the castle staff.

"Come to clean up, eh?"

The man straightened sharply, caught unawares.

"Sorry?"

"Clean up. Sweep, perhaps."

Maegor gestured generally around the hall, his chains of office clinking as he did. It was a gesture that took in the piles of rubble that filled the corners, the layer of red stone dust that covered everything and even the gaping holes in the roof left by the ravages of the departing dragon. Perhaps this would require a bit more than sweeping up. And the bearded fellow by the table didn't appear to have a broom. And, come to think of it, he looked too finely dressed and too noble of aspect to be a simple castle drudgeon.

"You're not here to clean up, are you?" said Maegor.

"Er, no," said the man and then smiled. He had very white teeth. He had all his teeth. It was rare to see a man over twenty years of age with all his teeth. It looked peculiar.

"You are...?" said Maegor.

"Almost constantly," said the man and came over to shake Maegor's hand. "Newport Pagnell. Delighted, I'm sure."

Maegor was master of seals, chief scribe to the king (or queen — matters were as yet undecided) and generally regarded as the wisest man in Grome and he didn't enjoy being on the backfoot with anyone. He wasn't sure who this Pagnell fellow was, why he was pumping his hand so vigorously or indeed whether it was Pagnell or himself who was supposed to be delighted.

Questions of who, why and whether were queuing up in Maegor's brain but were all interrupted by the arrival of the rest of the king's (or indeed queen's) privy council: Jynn the lord treasurer, Chrindle the master of horses and Cunnan the lord admiral.

"Ah, who's this long streak of nothing?" said Jynn, dropping bonelessly into the nearest chair.

"Another addition to the privy council?" said Chrindle, po-faced as always.

"The king clearly thinks we need another man at the table," said the grey-whiskered Cunnan.

"Which one?" said Jynn.

"Er, me?" said Pagnell.

"No, you pillock. Which king? We've got at least six thanes —"

"Seven," said Chrindle.

"Seven," said Jynn. "Down in what remains of the throne room, arguing over which of them should be king."

"Well, who doesn't want to be king?" said Pagnell.

Meagor and his fellow privy councillors all looked at Pagnell with firmly blank expressions.

"The six or seven thanes downstairs for one, I'd reckon," said Cunnan.

"Being king right now is like being handed a shitty stick," said Jynn.

"It is something of a...a poisoned chalice," Maegor said. "Hard and undoubtedly unpopular decisions lie ahead. Grome has been all but destroyed by dragonfire, its people variously dead, severely burned or —"

"Cooked to a medium rare," said Jynn cheerfully.

Maegor wrinkled his nose in disgust. Jynn's elevation to the role of lord treasurer had never been a good idea. The man was a thief, arguably the most successful thief in the city, but a common thief nonetheless. Just because he knew how to get hold of other people's money and keep hold of it did not mean he was suited to high office. His broken nose was a reminder to all of his low heritage. Jynn had not spent his life in studious preparation for civic service as Maegor had done.

Maegor tried to remember what he had been saying.

"Yes, the city is burned, the people are dead or wished they were. The old tyrant is dead, the dragon queen is dead —"

"And the dragon?" said Pagnell.

"Gone," said Cunnan. "Eastward."

Pagnell looked oddly pained by that news. He looked an

odd fellow anyway, not just because of his unnaturally whole smile. There was something about the sly look in his eyes, the sharp angle of his beard, the foreign cut of his clothing that made his coat and tunic not look quite like robes but…

"Are you some sort of wizard?" said Maegor.

"A more accurate description would be hard to express," said Pagnell.

"I knew a Yarwish wizard," said Cunnan, "back when I was plying the northern routes."

Maegor's opinion of Cunnan's suitability for his current role was not much higher than that he had of Jynn. Cunnan had a long history of being a sea trader but Maegor suspected there was more than a little piracy in that long career. 'Plying the northern routes' could have easily meant 'being an unholy terror on the northern seas'.

"The wizard's name was Tibshelf," said Cunnan. "You know him?"

"My old master," said Pagnell.

"Lost his left hand to hill tribes who thought they could gain his magic powers by eating him."

"His right hand," said Pagnell.

"Aye. Maybe it was," said Cunnan in the manner of one who thought he had set a clever trap and seen it avoided.

Cunnan took his seat opposite Chrindle.

Maegor pulled out a chair at the head of the table and brushed the dust from it before sitting. Even three days after the dragon had gone, ash and stone dust continued to fall on the city.

Pagnell hovered for a moment and then took one of the remaining chairs.

"Shall I? Here?"

"Please," said Maegor. "Our privy council now stands at five."

"With no king or queen to counsel," said Cunnan.

"Kings are expensive and over-rated," said Jynn. "Trust me."

"Can we get to business?" said Chrindle, armour plating clinking as she shifted in her seat. "This city cannot defend itself and we're wasting time. The dragon could return at any instant."

"Is that likely?" said Pagnell and looked to the massive holes in the ceiling above as though expecting to see a dragon swoop by at that moment.

"Inevitable, I should say," said Chrindle.

Maegor sighed. "You will have to forgive our master of horses. Charged with the defence of the city, she takes the dragon threat far too seriously."

"The master of seals does not take the threat seriously enough," Chrindle retorted fiercely. "If you look at the statistics —"

"Not today!" snapped Maegor. "We have other pressing matters. Now, if we could all turn our attention to the matter of how to feed and house the tens of thousands of displaced people currently milling about in our city's public spaces... I had my copyist draw up some lists and figures."

As Maegor dished out the parchment copies, he heard Pagnell lean over to Chrindle and say, "It's understandable to be worried. The dragon queen attacked once and you weren't prepared. It wasn't your fault, I'm sure."

Chrindle sat stiffly, saying nothing. Uncomfortable looks

passed between Jynn and Cunnan. Maegor cleared his throat and put down his papers.

"Pagnell. It is Pagnell, isn't it?"

"Yes?" said the wizard.

"When did you arrive in the city?"

"Yesterday."

"Ah." Maegor had hoped that 'Ah' would convey a lot more than it did and pressed on. "You perhaps are not fully aware of the state of things in Grome."

Pagnell looked round.

"Dragon queen turns up to conquer the city but instead burns it to the ground in a fit of rage, killing the old king, is turned on by one of her generals and... am I missing something?"

The silence that followed was long and horrible but Maegor could see the twitch in Chrindle's cheek and let her break the silence.

"I was the dragon queen's general," said Chrindle.

"Oh!" said Pagnell.

Cunnan raised a hand. "Her admiral."

"Ah, I see. And you two?" Pagnell gestured at Maegor and Jynn.

"A true servant of the kingdom," said Maegor.

"Enthusiastic local businessman," said Jynn.

Pagnell pretended to be impressed. He was a fair actor but Maegor was a better observer of people.

"And the two sides have come together to rebuild and reconcile."

"Not two sides as such," said Cunnan.

"The old king was a tyrant," said Maegor.

"A mad bastard," said Jynn.

"The dragon queen had a historical claim to the throne," said Chrindle.

"On her mother's side," said Maegor.

"I thought it was her aunt," said Cunnan.

"Her aunt on her mother's side."

"And the dragon queen had unified the peoples of the east," said Chrindle.

"In such a short time," Maegor agreed.

Jynn nodded. "It's amazing what a young woman with a dragon and long blonde tresses can achieve. Does a thing to a man, I can tell you, seeing her astride that beast."

"And so, we thought..."

"Yes, we thought..." said Chrindle.

"Aye," said Cunnan solemnly.

Pagnell look from one to the next, to the next, to the next. He did a little frown, licked his lips. A crazy little laugh escaped his lips.

"You invited the dragon queen to invade your capital city?"

No one wanted to speak but Cunnan eventually did.

"If you say it in that tone of voice, of course it's going to sound silly."

"It seemed logical at the time," said Maegor.

"And the king was a mad bastard," said Jynn. "Ran in the family."

"On his mother's side."

"Not his aunt?" said Cunnan.

"His mother, her aunt," said Maegor.

Pagnell nodded. "You invited the mad king's cousin —

the *hereditarily mad* king's cousin — to take the throne? With her dragon?"

"We were on her side."

"And she was on ours," said Jynn.

"Technically, if anything, it was *our* dragon," said Maegor.

"And how did that work out for you?" said Pagnell.

Maegor involuntarily looked around the ruins of the castle hall. Wind whistled through the shattered arches. Somewhere, in the distance, another ravaged building gave up and crumbled to the ground. If he listened hard enough, he imagined he could hear the thanes in the throne room below arguing about which one of the others should be king.

"I'm sure if we had the benefit of your wisdom two days ago, we could have avoided this," said Cunnan sourly.

"I do know a thing or two about dragons," said Pagnell.

"Like what?"

"They're wyrms. Flying wyrms. *Wyvernus wyvernus* or *draconis rex* to give them their proper names. Scales. Claws. Wings. Breathe fire."

"Aye, we know all this," said Cunnan.

"Some of us got to see that close up," said Jynn.

Chrindle gave the treasurer a pointed look.

"Some of us," said Jynn. "Didn't say it was me."

"They love gold," said Pagnell.

"Do they?" said Chrindle.

"Prudent business acumen?" said Jynn.

"They just do," said Pagnell. "I've heard it said that it's the softest flame-proof bedding material they can find but I've no evidence of that."

"And would the presence of gold draw dragons to the city?" asked Chrindle thoughtfully.

Maegor could see where the woman's train of thought was heading. It would lead to her dumping the city's wealth in the harbour to put it out of harm's way.

"The dragon is gone now," he said firmly.

"The damage is done," said Cunnan.

"So, let's deal with the matters at hand." He rustled his parchment meaningfully. "The injured, the starving, the homeless and the dispossessed. If we don't solve the first two then the last two won't matter."

"Oh, that's all right then," said Jynn.

"I meant that they are more urgent."

"If you like," said the treasurer. "But if the starving starved, we'd have fewer homeless. In fact, if we fed the starving on the injured..." A ready smile flashed. "There's plenty of barbecued bodies out there. I heard it tastes like pork."

"It doesn't," said Pagnell.

The privy council looked at the wizard.

"So, I hear," said Pagnell. "My old master Tibshelf had the unenviable experience of being offered a slice of his own severed hand."

"That's disgusting," said Chrindle.

"Cooked in a broth of mixed herbs I heard," said Cunnan.

"That does not make it better," said the master of horses.

"The matters at hand!" said Maegor with unconcealed annoyance.

"What hand?" said Jynn. "Oh, *at* hand. Starvation, death, blah, blah, blah."

"What else was I to assume?" said Maegor. "You see a fellow about the castle and you think 'servant'."

"Or thief," said Jynn.

"Quite," laughed Pagnell.

On a turn in the stairs, a chunk of wall was missing, its ragged edge blackened with soot. The city beyond was a black field dotted with the red light of fires.

"Camps of destitute souls across the city," said Maegor. "Huddling against the cold night."

"Those are camp fires," said Chrindle, pointing off to the north. "Those ones are just parts of the city that are still burning and haven't been put out."

"Couldn't the destitute just huddle by those fires?" suggested Jynn. "It'd save lighting new fires."

"Yes," said Maegor wearily. "I'll put it on the agenda for tomorrow."

2

Newport Pagnell's visit to Grome was not going entirely as he had hoped.

He had hoped to find more evidence of dragon presence (dragon dung, dragon eggs, even an actual dragon) rather than evidence of previous dragon occupation (fires, ruins, screaming people). He had clearly arrived a day too late. He had hoped it would be a simple in-out affair and that by now he would be on the road again, richer or wiser. He had not expected to be given a position on the privy council or the title of master of dragons. And he had certainly not expected to be given a luxurious room in the semi-ruined keep at the heart of the city.

Several times in the night, he poked his head out the door and found one of the royal red cloaks standing guard in the corridor. Each time, Pagnell had given the bloke a politely firm nod of greeting and returned to his room, to wait out the night.

Come the morning, the red cloak was still there but at least it now seem socially acceptable for Pagnell to be out and about so he gave one more politely firm nod of greeting and went exploring.

At the steps of the partially demolished tower at the southern corner of the castle, he found a broom, perhaps abandoned by someone who thought brooms were not up to the task of clearing this mess, perhaps even someone who had seen their broom as an analogy for the futility of human endeavour in the face of the wanton primal destruction and buggered off to seek a better life elsewhere. Pagnell picked up the broom and explored the tower further, confident now that anyone who saw him might assume he was a castle drudgeon about his business. In this way, the broom was merely a form of disguise but he did a little sweeping as he went, for what harm could it do?

A castle servant, a handsome if filthy young chap with a shock of blond hair, was hauling rubble down the stairs. He saw Pagnell approaching, opened his mouth to question him and then saw the broom and simply gave a nod as of one servant to another. The power of the broom was working!

"Now, where would a dragon roost?" Pagnell asked himself as he climbed the stairs. "If I were a visiting dragon, where would I make my nest?"

He had heard it from a number of sources that the dragon had taken up residence atop the South Tower. Pagnell inspected every level of this southern tower — abandoned rooms, web-filled corners and long forgotten spaces. He found an astronomical observatory, a bathroom containing a shattered porcelain bath and a unexpectedly large aviary (where cages were sadly occupied by a significant quantity of dead and mummified birds). Signs of dragon habitation were completely absent.

The information he'd gathered about the dragon was clearly duff. As he made his way back through the castle, he passed through the throne room where a number of Gromish thanes slept drunkenly at the trestle tables, exhausted by their arguing of the day before. He swept aside a couple of drinking horns and smiled at the guards as if he was meant to be there.

As he entered the hall of the privy council, he found the other members already there. Jynn and Chrindle sat at the table, one cleaning his fingernails with his knife, the other polishing her knife with a cloth. Maegor the scribe and Cunnan the sailor stood at a balcony overlooking the city. Pagnell joined them.

The city did not look much better in daylight. Smoke drifted across the streets. Various streets were just mounds of rubble.

"Contemplating the task ahead," Pagnell noted.

"Actually, we're watching them lads down there," said Cunnan and pointed.

A group of people, tiny figures when viewed from this height, were gathered along a long strip of bare earth. Several were cautiously stepping out onto it.

"The River Turge," said Maegor. "One of two that runs through the city."

"And the one that every man jack plus his wife, household and dog uses as their cesspit," said Cunnan. "It does not so much flow as ooze."

"Now, baked solid by dragonfire. If it's been, um, cooked all the way down then it will be quite solid."

A young man was edging further out onto the sandy brown surface.

"The smell's improved enormously," said Cunnan.

"We were debating whether to have it paved over," said Maegor. "Have it buried underground."

"There are better things to spend the city's money on," said Chrindle.

"Yes, yes," said Maegor, ambling back to the table. The man's heavy chains, symbols of his learning, hung heavily about him, defining his gait. Pagnell was unimpressed. One of the few advantages of symbolism was that symbols didn't have to weigh anything. If your symbols were an actual physical burden then someone had made a bad design choice somewhere along the line.

The privy council were called to order. Pagnell put his broom to one side. Cunnan gave him a questioning look.

"Thought I might make myself useful as I wandered around the castle," said Pagnell.

"And what were you doing wandering around the castle?" said Chrindle.

"Looking for dragons," he said and smiled to show he was joking, which he wasn't.

"The dragon has gone," Maegor pointed out.

"Ah, but they do lay dragon eggs and from them mighty dragons do grow."

"We must discuss the city's defences today," said Chrindle.

Maegor grumbled and rearranged his papers. Pagnell

could see that the master of seals maintained his position as chair of the meeting by having the most paperwork in front of him. In a successful bureaucracy, he who controls the paperwork, controls the world.

"We must indeed discuss matters of expenditure," he said. "The destruction of the city presents us with one significant opportunity: the chance to rebuild Grome as the city it should be rather than the city it was."

"I liked the city as it was," said Jynn.

"I'm sure you did," said Maegor. "All those twisting alleys and dead ends. The city was like a rabbit warren."

"Our priority," said Chrindle, "should be the defence of the city."

"Maegor and I were discussing sanitation," said Cunnan. "The digging of sewers. The sinking of wells."

"Is that important right now?"

"I would like to live in a city where people do not throw their slops out into the street," said Maegor.

"Nothing wrong with that," said Jynn. "Keeps you on your toes."

"Cleanliness is important," Pagnell pointed out. "Keeps a population healthy. Extends life."

"Take a look at some of those poor buggers out there," said Jynn. "You think they want their lives extending?"

"If we want to keep the populace alive then we must build up our defences," said Chrindle. "We must prepare for another dragon attack."

"Gods preserve us all," said Maegor, exasperated. "The dragon is gone. We are talking about saving the people from plague."

"How many people died of plague in the city last year?" said Chrindle.

"We've had this argument before, dear lady."

"How many?"

"Specifically of plague, eight hundred."

"And the dragon killed?"

"Our best guess would be somewhere around nine thousand," said Cunnan.

"Dragons kill ten times as many people as plague," said Chrindle.

"Eleven times," said Pagnell.

"But that was a one-time incident," said Cunnan.

"But it only happened three days ago," said Chrindle, "so on average that's…"

"Three thousand dragon-related deaths a day," said Pagnell.

"Precisely," said Chrindle.

"But up until now there's never been a dragon attack on Grome," said Maegor.

"Maybe this is a sign of things to come."

"There might not be another one for another ten years, though."

"That would still be nine hundred dragon-related deaths per year on average," said Pagnell. "More than plague."

"You are not helping," said Maegor through gritted teeth.

"Sorry. I can't resist arithmetic," Pagnell admitted.

"It remains a leading cause of death in the city and we should prepare," said Chrindle, emphasising a point with a thump of her fist on the table that sent her iron arm greaves ringing. Why the woman was wearing armour to a meeting was slightly beyond Pagnell although he suspected that either she was one of those people who wanted to be prepared for every eventuality at every moment or, as a woman in a man's world, she wanted the most obvious signs of her womanhood to be buried under several layers.

"As master of horses, what do you recommend?" said Maegor.

"Giant crossbows to be positioned every fifty yards along the city walls."

"Fanciful nonsense."

"Actually, the Satheans have made siege engine crossbows a successful addition to their army," said Pagnell. "It's improved their effectiveness in the field of combat enormously."

"See?" said Chrindle.

"It's true that they're notoriously capricious machines. The string are prone to breaking and, when they do, the recoil from the string is liable to behead anyone within ten yards."

"And how is that supposed to improve combat effectiveness?" scoffed Cunnan.

"The siege crossbow crews are entirely made up of soldiers who have shown cowardice in battle. Nothing instils bravery like the threat of random bowstring decapitation. I have seen these devices myself and I have some experience with the construction of siege engines. There was this one time when some tribespeople mistook me for a salt-witch and —"

"No giant crossbows," said Maegor.

"We can't afford them," agreed Jynn.

"Then we arm and train the general populace in the use of longbows," said Chrindle. "If we can't kill a dragon with a giant crossbow, we can at least drive it off with a thousand arrows."

"How will we train them?" said Cunnan.

"Sounds expensive," agreed Jynn.

"Make it the law. An hour's practice a day for every man, woman and child in the kingdom."

"And the expense of enforcing that law?" said Jynn doubtfully.

"Set up regional archery contests," suggested Pagnell. "Small prizes. Promise a grand competition by year's end. Do you have a national sport?"

"Jousting?" suggested Chrindle.

"Dice?" offered Jynn.

"Archery it is then. You have a national hero?"

"Eh?" said Cunnan.

"Someone you sing ballads about."

"Not in the ballads I know," said Jynn.

"There are a few celebrated kings and queens," said Maegor.

"Probably not popular at the moment," said Pagnell. "May I suggest your new national hero be, um, Brad Bowman."

"Who?" said Chrindle.

"Or whatever his — or her! — name might be. The legendary local hero who sent the dragon fleeing by — why did the dragon leave?"

"My guess would be boredom," said Cunnan.

"Stormed off in a fit of pique after his queen was slain," said Maegor.

"Nothing left to burn?" said Jynn.

"Well," said Pagnell, "in your new narrative, it was a solitary arrow from Brad Bowman's bow —"

"I've never heard of him," said Chrindle.

"No, I know," said Pagnell patiently. "We're constructing his myth now."

"I'm just saying that if we're going to be spinning stories, shouldn't it be about someone famous."

"He will be. For driving off the dragon. A story to inspire the Gromish to take up a new sport, a new weapon to protect the realm from enemies foreign and draconic."

"The Yarwish have adopted this system already," said Cunnan.

"Finest longbowmen in the world if I do say so myself," said Pagnell.

Maegor looked uncomfortable.

"Trust me," said Pagnell. "You'd never want to face a Yarwishman in a shooting contest."

"My concern," said the master of seals, "is putting such, er, military power in the hands of the peasant classes. How do the Yarwish kings rule if every subject can take up arms against him?"

"Carefully," said Pagnell.

The members of the privy council looked at one another and then, recognising that none of them were of royal blood and recalling what poor experience they had had with kings and queens of late, gave a collective shrug and mumbled assent.

"Dragon drills," said Chrindle.

"What?" said Cunnan.

"Dragon drills. Every week, to prepare us for —"

"No," said Maegor.

"I have designs for a dragon-shaped kite and fire lanterns that will —"

"No." Maegor was firm. "We had enough trouble caused by crocodile drills."

"Crocodile drills?" said Pagnell.

Maegor closed his eyes and shook his head. "The last queen. Mad as a sack of fairies. It's a pathetic tale. No. No dragon drills."

Chrindle huffed. "None of you are willing to spend coin —"

"Coin we haven't got, love," said Jynn.

"No simple defences. No giant crossbows. No dragon drill. Spikes on the roofs of buildings?"

"That could be reasonable," said Maegor.

"Thirty foot spikes of beaten steel."

"Ah, not three inch spikes of bog iron then?"

"We're dealing with a dragon, not pigeons. What about the creation of fire breaks across the city?"

"And that would be?"

"Open areas with no buildings in so that should — *when* a dragon attacks, the fire won't spread from building to building across the entire city."

"Like parks, then," said Cunnan.

"If you wish."

"To protect the city, we should avoid rebuilding parts of it?" said Maegor. "Will that cost us anything?"

"Not building things tends to be quite cheap," said Jynn.

"And will provide open spaces for the practising of archery," said Pagnell.

Maegor dipped his quill in ink and put a big tick on the parchment in front of him.

3

Digesting a lunch of fresh bread and beer, Pagnell stood with his fellow privy councillors and observed the men on the baked River Turge. The distant figures were getting bolder now.

"Bet you a crown that one makes it to the other side," said Jynn.

"Would that we had time to waste in watching," said Maegor.

"I suppose," said Pagnell after some thought, "that could be carved up and burned as fuel."

"Burned turds?" said Jynn.

"If the eastern tribes can burn horse dung..." said Cunnan.

A timid fellow in scribe's robes entered and passed Maegor a sealed scroll. Maegor opened it and read and then cursed softly.

"And they brought you this just, Zirocks?"

The young man nodded and was dismissed with a wave.

"Our duty is never done," said Maegor and directed them all back to the table.

"But I would have a wager on those mudskippers down there," said Jynn.

"There will be other men and other wagers," said Maegor.

"We were discussing the imposition of a curfew in the city," said Chrindle as they sat.

"That may have to wait."

"But there is widespread looting at night."

"Is it looting," said Jynn, "when people are simply picking up what they find in the street?"

"I think it's poor justice for a fellow if he has thrown his worldly goods out of his front window to save them from the fire, only for passers-by to take them," said Cunnan.

"But does the law not say 'finders keepers'?"

"It does not," said Chrindle firmly.

"Perhaps it ought to," said Jynn. "Any man not wise enough to hide his gold probably doesn't deserve to own any."

"And on the subject of gold, Master Pagnell was telling me that gold has a 'specific gravity' and I am more and more concerned that it will pull in fresh dragons."

"It's... it's not that kind of gravity," said Pagnell. "I don't think it really matters —"

"It does not matter," said Maegor. "We have this fresh matter to deal with." He waved the scroll.

"What matter?" said Cunnan.

"The dead bodies in the street."

"Hardly fresh," said Jynn and chuckled at his own jest.

Maegor scowled at him. Pagnell watched the silent interplay between the privy councillors. Maegor as representative of tradition and the old ways, Jynn as representative of the new thrusting and dynamic nature of society (thrusting with concealed daggers and dynamically relieving people of their purses, if Pagnell was any judge). Chrindle and Cunnan as pragmatic moderates, one who saw the world as a fight between 'them' and 'us', the other seeing the web of trade and culture that tied Grome to the world.

"A delegation has been sent from the twelve temples in the city," said Maegor.

"Priests working together," said Cunnan. "Wonders shall never cease."

"Wonders are their business," said Pagnell.

"As is disposing of the dead," said Maegor. "There are several thousand corpses in the city and the priesthood have declared that there will be room in their graveyards, crypts and ossuaries for them all."

"That's all good then," said Jynn.

"*But,*" said Maegor, "their services do not come for free."

"Pardon?" said Chrindle.

"They want paying. And so they have formed a collective bargaining organisation, a union, and have written a list of demands — and, yes, I believe I recognise the hand of the high priestess of Buqit on this parchment."

"They want paying to bury stiffs?" said Jynn. "With the numbers we've got, we should just have a big pit dug and tip the bodies in. Job done."

"And the priests, foreseeing your suggestion," said

Maegor, "have predicted that the gods will be most angry with this sacrilegious treatment of the righteous dead. Divine retribution has been hinted at."

"Dragons!" whispered Chrindle fearfully.

"Unspecified," said Maegor.

"The bodies do need disposing of," said Pagnell. "Reverentially, I mean. And, one supposes, they would have been disposed of at some point anyway, dragon or no dragon."

"What do you mean?" said Cunnan.

Pagnell smiled gently. "Everyone dies eventually. And if they had died of natural causes, would it have been the family who would have paid?"

"It would," said Jynn.

"But whole families have been turned to ash by the dragon," said Chrindle.

"And become a burden to the crown."

"And how much do the temples charge?" said Pagnell.

Maegor unrolled his scroll further. "They have kindly provided us with a sliding scale from high ranking nobles to paupers."

"I think, given that those who died either had no home or were destroyed along with their house," said Jynn, "we could argue most convincingly that all the dead are paupers."

"But many of the dead are naught but ash and charcoal," said Cunnan. "If we are to pay per body, how are we to distinguish one from another?"

"Skulls?" said Maegor.

Pagnell who had seen what dragonfire could do to a body

on his way into the city doubted that there would necessarily be many skulls to be found.

"Weight," he said.

"For what?" said Chrindle.

He tutted. "We pay them by weight. If it is a penny per pauper then we pay them a penny for a pauper's-weight of human remains."

"A penny is probably optimistic," said Maegor.

"And — and! —" said Pagnell, excited by a sudden idea, "given that the wealthier the individual the more portly and corpulent they are likely to be then the more we will be paying for them proportionally."

"Although much of that portliness is fat," mused Maegor (who was not a thin man himself). "Tallow for the candles."

"Are you suggesting the fat and wealthy burn better?" said Jynn.

"It's funny where idle thoughts take you."

By the look on her face, Chrindle did not think it funny. A soldier, she had perhaps seen enough of death to think it distasteful or perhaps not think anything of it at all.

"Speaking of temples," said Cunnan, "there are now, I believe, thirteen temples in the city."

"Oh?" said Chrindle.

"Folks are calling the new one the Temple of the Dragon."

"Oh, I walked past that. Down by the banks of the Turge. I thought it was a restaurant. Or a brothel."

"It does have a certain gaudy quality about it, aye."

"I was concerned about the amount of gold leaf they were using on the statue out front."

The woman was obsessed with the dangerous dragon-luring effects of gold.

"And what are the principal tenets of this new faith?" asked Jynn innocently. Pagnell could hear the innocent tone in his voice, the deliberately innocent tone.

"It seems they believe that the dragon is a god," said Cunnan.

"Blasphemy," said Maegor.

"Maybe. But it does live in the sky and it does visit ruin on those who displease it."

"Not distinguishing between wicked and virtuous," Maegor pointed out.

"Aye, sounds like a god to me. And they say that if you give gold to the Temple of the Dragon then you'll be protected from its wrath."

"And people believe that?"

"Well, the priests are keen to point out that the building housing the temple was not burned down in the dragon attack, so..."

"But the temple only came into existence after the dragon attack," said Pagnell. "So, they simply set up in one of the buildings that was left standing."

Cunnan itched his grey whiskers. "The people of Grome are many fine things. Intelligent is not one of them."

The remainder of the afternoon was devoted to dealing with many of the unresolved issues on Maegor's agenda. A decree was worded to the effect that any new buildings in the city should be constructed of non-flammable and therefore hopefully dragon-proof material. Plans for reopening trade routes with neighbouring cities were discussed and orders put into place from clearing the charred shipwrecks that currently blocked the harbour. It was decided that 'dragon courts' would be set up to resolve disputes over who owned what — including houses, possessions and corpses — in this crazy post-dragon city. Each of the privy councillors went away with tasks to do and their own minions to muster.

Pagnell loitered as Maegor and his copyist, Zirocks, tidied and tried to make sense of all the scribbles and notations made that day.

"I wondered if you would like me to take a look at the priests' proposals," said Pagnell. "I could do some calculations regarding body weights and the relative social status of the corpse."

"You know how much a burned body weighs?" said Maegor.

"Give me a set of weighing scales, a sausage and pot to cook it in and I could make an intelligent guess."

Maegor smiled. "You are a very clever man, aren't you?"

"Too clever for my own good sometimes," the wizard agreed. "By the way, I suspect your lord treasurer has a controlling share or at least some stake in the Temple of the Dragon."

"I suspect it too," said Maegor. "As long as they pay their taxes I might be disinclined to care." He moved to the balcony. "It must be somewhere over... there."

Maegor pointed past the rock solid Turge River on which young men now boldly strolled. Pagnell couldn't be sure exactly where Maegor thought it might be.

"If it has a gold-plated statue of a dragon outside, I'm

surprised no one's tried to destroy it as some belated form of revenge," said Maegor.

"Or steal it," said Pagnell.

"It would be worth something."

"Not as much as a real dragon. Dead or alive."

"Or even just a dragon egg."

"Or even just the shell," said Pagnell before he could stop himself.

"Oh, but people will believe that stealing that statue would make the dragon god angry," said Maegor.

"It's funny what people believe."

Maegor appeared to be about to disagree and then changed his mind.

"The king's — the late king's great aunt believed she was destined to be eaten by a crocodile."

"The queen? Mad as a sack of fairies?"

"That was her," said Maegor.

"Mad monarchs tend to believe all manner of foolish things."

"Odd thing was, she was right."

"Really?" said Pagnell.

4

THE QUEEN AND THE CROCODILE

It was told to me thus [said Maegor].

The king's great aunt, the queen, was obsessed by the belief that she would one day be killed by a crocodile. It was, without doubt, her greatest fear.

A crocodile. A legged river serpent, with scaly armoured plate and in possession of a mouth like a trapdoor full of sharp teeth. They crave the sun's warmth and, if exposed to the cold, become sluggish and lifeless.

Yes, we do live in a more temperate corner of the world. A crocodile would find life here far too chilly. And indeed that did make the queen's fear a little unusual. This was compounded by the fact that she believed the crocodile in question — her inescapable doom — would find her in the bath.

She was mad, of course. Though I would not have said so at the time. Who am I to question the mind of a monarch? I may be a scribe and the advisor to the throne but I knew my place. But I did try to counsel the woman.

I queried her belief and pointed out the more obvious flaws in the notion.

She said to me, "Maegor, I feel it is true in my very bones. And there is, of course, precedence. I recall most clearly being bitten in the bath as a child."

"Bitten?" I said. "By a crocodile?"

The queen gave me a thoughtful look. "I do not remember if it was a crocodile specifically but in my mind's eye, I see a dark shape, those foul red eyes and feel — oh, I feel it now, Maegor! — sharp teeth nipping at my toes."

I did not dismiss the queen's comment out of hand, but I asked if she might have misremembered the event.

"I would imagine," I added, "that the appearance of a crocodile in the young princess's bath tub would be quite a story and be remembered by many of the older members of castle staff. I have asked around…"

The queen waved my objections away with her fan.

"They can barely remember anything from one day to the next. The cook can't remember how I like my eggs salted, and when I ask the maid of my chamber for my favourite dress…"

"Yes, your majesty," I said, "but, a crocodile… I mean, *a crocodile*. I am certain it would stick in the mind."

And she gave me one of those looks. A wise man does not ignore such a look. I did not question her further that day. It is the monarch's prerogative to think as he or she wishes. If the monarch says up is down, the moon is the sun or that his army must make war against the rainclouds then so be it. Yes, that last was the old king's father. There are still holes in the roof of the northwest turret tower from where a catapult's load went astray.

The king's father, the queen's nephew, comes into this story of course. For, just as the queen felt it was her destiny to be eaten by a crocodile in the bathtub, so he felt it was his destiny to become king, his duty even. He was of the opinion that if his mad aunt — his words at the time, not mine — were to meet her grisly end then it should be sooner rather than later. Why so pressing?

The queen was to marry.

A suitor had been chosen, a prince from some far off kingdom. A marriage might soon lead to children and, then, the queen's nephew would no longer be next in line to the throne. He resolved to put his plan into action before the prince even arrived. Oh, we can speak of it now. We live in strange times and, besides, regicide, as long as it's done by close family, is part of the natural order of things. Meanwhile, while he plotted to assassinate the queen, I resolved to tackle another matter most pressing.

You see, the queen so feared finding a crocodile in her bathtub that she had not bathed, to my knowledge, since childhood. There might have been a little light washing of various bits as and when they became available but the queen was more inclined to mask her, um, her natural aroma with scents and oils. Oh, the noble folk do smell far sweeter than we common soil but — how should I put this? — the queen had *accumulated* more than a little filth over the years. Oh, it fell off her in clods, your majesty. We have a surprisingly large example in the family chapel.

The queen needed a bath. Her groom-to-be might have been a noble of lesser standing, but no matter his status, his ardour or his state of intoxication, a man expects certain standards on his wedding night.

I approached the matter gently.

"How," I asked the queen, "do you imagine a crocodile might get into your bath?"

"Well," she replied, in the manner of one who had thought about it at length, "I expect it will come up through the pipes."

"Pipes?" I asked.

"Yes, Maegor. The pipes that carry the water."

"They are quite small," I pointed out.

"I imagine crocodiles are very squishable," she replied. "Bones made of rubber or some such."

"Yes," I said. "I can look into that but I'm very much given to understand that crocodiles are both gargantuan in size and, in no sense at all 'squishable'."

"Or up the toilet," said the queen.

"We can block the toilet for the duration of your bath. We could have your heaviest maid sit on it."

"Or perhaps," she said shrewdly, "the crocodile is already there."

"Pardon, your majesty?" I said.

"It's already there. Maybe it entered my bath chamber as a baby crocodile — or an egg! — and then proceeded to grow."

I was speechless for a moment and I rarely am such.

"Your majesty," I queried gently, "you are suggesting that the enormous crocodile that you fear is already in your bathtub and has been there for several years, growing? I am confident that someone would have spotted it before now. Or, indeed, been eaten by it."

"Perhaps they have. We do have a lot of servants. If one or two went missing, who would notice?"

I attempted a different approach.

"Your majesty," I said, "even if any of this were true, why would a crocodile be here, thousands of miles from its tropical home?"

"Perhaps it escaped from a travelling menagerie," she said promptly.

"Menageries and zoological exhibits have been banned throughout the kingdom on your command for that very reason," I said.

"A dealer in rare pets!"

"No, your majesty."

"Or... someone who wishes me harm might procure one and... and... encase it in ice to send it to sleep – they do sleep when cold, do they not? – and then place it in my bathtub to defrost."

The queen was most pleased with this explanation, but it was up to me to bring her back to reality.

"Your majesty," I humbly began, "the chances of you being eaten by a crocodile are remote beyond comprehension. You are far more likely to simply drown in your tub or slip on a bar of soap and crack open your skull."

"Nonsense!" she scoffed. "So tawdry a death! So banal! Do you forget who you speak to?"

I retreated hastily but, over the weeks to come, I chipped away at her resolve. A bath before her wedding day was essential and I knew in my heart that her life was not in danger.

I consider myself a man of subtle persuasions. I endeavour to rip back the veil of folly and reveal the path of wisdom to all who will listen. The queen consented to a bath at last.

Oh, she put up a struggle. She insisted on a number of 'crocodile drills'. The entire household was instructed what to do in the event of a loose crocodile. Certain doors were identified as 'emergency exits' and marked with plaques bearing the image of a figure pursued by a crocodile. Certain stewards were nominated as 'crocodile marshals' with the role of guiding people out and ensuring all were accounted for. A unit of the palace guard was designated as the Royal Crocodoons, given their own unique livery and equipped with an array of weapons that the master of arms thought best for fighting crocodiles.

It was a mistake to concede to the queen's request that, during the crocodile drills, one servant was dressed up as the offending beast and instructed to run up and down the corridors, roaring and flapping its ridiculous jaws. Yes, the queen had sent to Carius for the eviscerated remains of a crocodilian — a sad and flaky specimen that was coming apart at the seams, I recall. Between drills, she insisted the crocodile be placed in her bedchamber.

She was mad, you see. I did say. The old king's father said it and he was right. She stared at her nemesis for hours with horrified fascination. Shortly before she took her bath, I approached to offer words of encouragement and I found her staring into the dull black eyes of the beast, hypnotised.

Whatever came next, her mind had already been consumed.

"I hear," she said faintly, "that the peoples of the far south revere the crocodile as a god, a thing to be feared and respected."

The queen retreated to her bath chamber alone to take her bath.

I was not there at the end. Of course not. There are certain facts I can tell you and my own reverie of how the queen would have met her death. The facts then: there was no crocodile in there before she entered, the toilet and garderobe chute below were securely sealed. At no point did the queen cry out. The maid outside the room thought she heard the queen mutter a handful of words but could not be sure.

My thoughts? The queen undressed to bathe. Her stinking clothes, mired with the grime of years, were found draped over a chair. And then, at some point, she saw the crocodile. Oh, what a beast. Any man would feel honoured to have such a monster attend the moment of his demise. Twenty feet of muscly death, every inch of it armoured in green-black studs of horny plate. A mouth as deep as your arm is long, as wide as your head. Teeth like diamond shards. Picture it. Picture that open maw, its tongue, wet and pink, waiting to taste you. Eyes? No glint of demonic fire in those eyes, no cruel intent, but a cold yellow gaze with an indifference that would make you tremble.

The queen could have screamed for what good it would have done her but she did not. Was she struck dumb? No.

The maid outside reported after that she thought she heard the queen say, "No, not like this," or something similar.

I think it was then that the queen stepped into the bath and sat among the steam and scented soap bubbles. She had declared that she would be eaten by a crocodile in her bath and, I think, was determined that it should be so. To be eaten by a crocodile was not enough. A true monarch knows that their word and their authority trumps all other things. Better to be dead than fallible.

The crocodile put its clawed feet on the edge of the bath and hauled its great bulk over the rim. The queen's body was all aquiver. Whose wouldn't be? She raised one foot daintily in encouragement. It obligingly opened its mouth. A fast and savage chomp or a delicate nibble, I couldn't tell you. As I say, she did not scream once.

The prince arrived the following day and left, unwed, the day after that. And the queen's nephew, the old king's father, was crowned king.

How did the crocodile get into the bathroom? I have absolutely no idea. The new king? No, not at all. That's a ridiculous notion. The queen's nephew had hired a foreign assassin to slit the queen's throat and lost his deposit when it turned out no throat slitting would be necessary.

A king? Use a crocodile to kill someone? Of course not. He wasn't mad.

5

"You made that up," said Pagnell.

"I did not," said Maegor. "On my word of honour."

"Crocodoons?"

"Crocodoons. Absolutely."

Pagnell shook his head but said nothing more.

There was a shout from far below, little more than a mewl at this distance. Pagnell and Maegor looked down at the dusky streets. On the dried River Turge a hole had appeared, such as a fork might make in a pie crust. From the hole steam drifted and something bubbled. Of the man who had made the hole in the crust, there was no sign.

"There are worse deaths than being eaten by a crocodile," suggested Maegor.

Pagnell raised the papers with the priests' demands on it.

"I will have your calculations for you by tomorrow," he said and made to go.

"Don't forget your broom," said Maegor.

"Ah."

Pagnell picked up his broom and took to the stairs.

The thanes were arguing in the throne room again. Pagnell paused to listen.

"Who do you have your money on?" said Jynn, appearing from the shadows. He was half a head taller than Pagnell and when the man loomed — he was one of life's loomers — his broken nose and the story it hinted at loomed large with him. Pagnell saw the man's hand resting casually on the hilt of his dagger.

Pagnell took a step back.

"I don't think... that is, I'm not a betting man."

Jynn grinned. "Oh, I think you are a risk-taker, wizard. That's undeniable."

Pagnell took a step sideways towards the throne room. A step back, a step to the side — he was a knight's move away from being free of this slippery and dangerous man.

"I think the city is coping admirably without a king," he said.

"Someone has to wear the crown," said Jynn. "The crown looks silly all by itself. You need a man to wear the crown. You need a crown to identify the king. You see the crown and you know where you are."

"Er, yes."

Jynn nodded at the broom in Pagnell's hand. "It's like brooms."

"Is it?"

"You walk around with a broom in your hand, people think you're a sweep."

"I suppose so."

"You walk around with a broom in your hand and, because people think you're a sweep, they don't stop to question who you are or where you're going."

"No?"

"Oldest trick in the book."

"Or I could just have been doing some sweeping," said Pagnell.

Jynn gave him a look. "Unlikely though, ain't it?"

Pagnell stepped — once, twice — gave the lord treasurer a nod of farewell and fled to his room. There was a red cloak on guard outside.

Pagnell went inside and bolted the door. He emerged half an hour later with a scroll. "Could you be a good man," he said to the red cloak, "and tell me who is the most popular bard in the city?"

"Bard?"

"Street entertainer, pub singer, whatever."

"There's a lute player who always coins it in at the Crossroads Inn, I suppose, sir."

"And is it still standing?"

"The lute player?"

"The inn. Well, both."

"I believe so, sir. I would say that her songs are sometimes a bit on the vulgar side."

"Excellent."

"There's this one, *Who Blew the Red Cloak's Whistle?*, and it's meant to be about a whistle but really, I think, if you think about it —"

"Yes, yes. Sounds perfect. Go give her that. Bring her back here if you can."

"Yes, sir."

"And a sausage."

"Sausage?"

"Yes. An uncooked sausage, please."

"Right you are, sir."

The red cloak turned to go but Pagnell gripped his arm.

"And when you return, you will be on guard here all night long, won't you?"

"Yes, my lord."

"Good-o," said Pagnell. "As long as I know you're keeping me nice and safe."

"I mean, not all of us red cloaks are even issued with whistles."

"That must be a great disappointment to you."

Pagnell closed the door, bolted it and then dragged a chair in front of it. He thought about it a little longer and then shuttered the window.

6

Cunnan walked into the privy council hall. It was a grey and cold morning outside, made greyer by the ash and soot that still predominated in the streets. The hall was cold, being open to the sky and, at his age, having spent most of his life on the mostly single or double storey decks of ships, he did not relish the number of stairs he had to climb each day to reach it. Nonetheless, he was in cheery mood. This might have been because he had spent a very entertaining evening in the local tavern. It might have been because his frequently bad back had allowed him a full night's sleep for once. Or it might just have been that he had discovered long ago that there was almost nothing to be gained from being miserable and had resolved that cheerfulness should be his default mood.

"You're humming," said Chrindle, as he approached the table.

Cunnan realised that indeed he had been.

"Aye," he said, "a little ditty I heard Lady Forge singing in the tavern. Someone has been busy, I'd say."

He looked along the table at Maegor, Pagnell and Jynn.

"*How sharp Brad's eye! The arrow did fly and struck the dragon true!*" sang Cunnan.

Pagnell waved his hands, pretending to be embarrassed.

"It was just a little something. A collaborative piece Lady Forge and I knocked up together last night."

"You and Lady Forge?" said Jynn, impressed.

"A commission, if you will," said the wizard. "Mostly based on an old Yarwish air."

"They'll all be singing *The Ballad of Brad Bowman* by tonight," said Cunnan approvingly. "I mean, it's no *Who Blew the Red Cloak's Whistle?* but still —"

"Red cloaks don't even carry whistles," said Chrindle. "They keep asking me if they can have them."

"To raise the alarm on the discovering of thieves and such," nodded Maegor.

"They tell me people are making fun of them if they say they haven't got one," said Chrindle, mystified.

Cunnan smiled.

"What?" said Chrindle.

"Nothing," he said. "I'm just a cheerful soul."

"Rumours are circulating," said Jynn. "Stories of this Brad Bowman. Friend of a friend saw him kind of thing."

"Then it's working," said Pagnell.

"When I was in the tavern, I also heard," said Cunnan, "that there's a wizard in the city who will pay a bounty on any dragon bits people might find."

"Bits?" said Chrindle.

"Dislodged scales. Bits of claw."

"Or even dragon egg shell?" said Maegor archly, with a look directed at Pagnell.

The wizard blustered. "I'm a keen scholar. What can I say?"

"You need these things for some sorcerer's brew?" said Cunnan.

"They have their uses," Pagnell conceded. "Can't a man honestly seek rare and efficacious materials?"

"I don't know," said Jynn. "Can he?"

"But if we throw suspicions on every man who tried to make a little profit on the side, we would never get anything done," said Cunnan.

"True enough," said Jynn although Cunnan could see that Chrindle — ever honest, ever dutiful — didn't agree.

"Then let us deal with more pressing business," said Maegor. "A union delegation visited the castle first thing this morning."

"The priests again?" said Chrindle.

"No, but we'll come to them in good time, I'm sure. These delegates were from the Union of Charcoal Burners and Allied Trades."

"Never heard of them."

"And that would be because they didn't exist until yesterday. It would seem that, encouraged by the example of the priests, the charcoal burners of Grome have unionised and come to us to plead their case."

"What case?" said Jynn.

"That they have been done a grievous disservice by the dragon."

"I think we've all been disserviced by the dragon."

"Ah, but they claim to have been disserviced — disserviced? Disserved? — doubly so."

"Doubly so? How so?"

"Thus. While many homes and businesses have been destroyed by the dragon, most

individuals have only lost their homes and livelihoods to the fire."

"But the charcoal burners...?"

"Have been insulted twice over because the wood buildings and structures of the city —"

"Have been reduced to charcoal," nodded Pagnell.

"The product of their labours is now abundant and essentially free to all."

"The market's been flooded," said Jynn and laughed. "Oh, it's funny. Admit it."

"Says a man who's never been in fear of his livelihood vanishing," said Cunnan and then reflected that much of Jynn's livelihood probably relied on him vanishing at the right moment, specifically at the moment when his victims realised they had been robbed.

"What do they expect us to do about it?" said Chrindle.

"Pay reparations," said Maegor simply. "Recompense them for earnings lost."

Chrindle scoffed. "They want paying for charcoal they would have sold if the dragon hadn't done their job for them? Fie! And I suppose the red cloaks should be paid for the bandits and thieves they would have caught if the dragon had not done away with them?"

"I had personally always thought that known thieves

should be paid to not make a nuisance of themselves," said Jynn. "Or to keep their thievery within reasonable levels."

Maegor scowled fiercely at that notion and opened his mouth to offer a rebuttal when the wizard Pagnell spoke.

"The city still needs charcoal."

"It does," said Cunnan.

"And, as I understand, charcoal doesn't go 'off'."

"I'm no expert but no."

"Then during these times of... abundance, perhaps the crown might be willing to put some charcoal aside, to stockpile it."

"And why would the crown want to do that?"

"Most of the wooden buildings in the city have been turned to charcoal."

"Aye," said Cunnan.

"And we have already drawn up estimates for the cost of clearing those ruined sites."

"Yes," said Jynn.

"But if the Union of Charcoal Burners and Allied Trades would consider, temporarily at least, becoming the Union of Charcoal *Collectors* and Allied Trades then we would get those ruined sites cleared in no time."

"But the charcoal burners still want paying," said Maegor.

"Charcoal burning is a skill, almost mystical. Charcoal collecting...?" Pagnell made a sad hum of a noise. "Less so. We can agree a price that the crown would be willing to meet for every hundredweight of charcoal."

"It's still an expense," said Jynn.

"Ah, but as the charcoal supply is transferred to our care,

the abundant product becomes scarcer, the price to the consumer rises and…"

"… and the crown sits on a mountain of the stuff to be sold off at whatever price the market can bear," said Jynn, nodding eagerly. "On top of which, we should insist that all members of the union take out dragon insurance to protect them in future."

"Dragon insurance?" said Chrindle.

"It's a new concept that some clever bloke in the city came up with," said Jynn and Cunnan wondered if the 'clever bloke' in question was Jynn himself. "It works like this. You pay the insurer a premium, an amount of money and, in exchange, he promises that if whatever it is you've insured gets destroyed or stolen then he will pay for it."

"Why pay the money to another man if you can pay for the repairs or replacement yourself?" said Chrindle.

"No, you misunderstand. The premium you pay is less than the cost of repairs."

"Then why would the insurer enter into the deal? He'd be a fool to take less money than the cost of the works needed doing. Any craftsman who sold his wares for less than they cost to make would be out on the street in no time."

"You don't understand," said Jynn.

"You're not explaining," Chrindle retorted.

"It's very simple."

"So it should be simple to explain."

"It's like… It's like…" Jynn waved his arms about in search of inspiration. "Gods! It's like the gods!"

Cunnan steepled his fingers and leaned forward, interested.

"Let's say you were a trader and you had a ship due in," said Jynn. "It's out at sea and there's tell of storms. You might go down to the temple and make an offering to Pedlo the crab-limbed god of the sea."

"Oh, no," said Cunnan. "That's a basic error. I always make my offerings to Diamé, goddess of good fortune and propitious outcomes. Covers all bases."

"Not Lekki? If it's storms you fear then the god of lightning would be my go-to god."

"Regardless," said Jynn, "you would make an offering of food, a sacrifice —"

"I always make an offering of coin," said Cunnan.

"Do you?" said Chrindle.

"In my experience, you give someone a gift, they might not want it. Give them money and they can spend it on what they like."

"Point is," said Jynn, "you've made some sort of outlay — it's cost you — but it's not as much as the value of the cargo on your ship."

"Of course not. That would be foolish."

"And maybe the ship wasn't going to sink in a storm anyway, but you made an offering to the gods nonetheless. The gods are happy, your ship comes in and everyone's happy. See?"

There were careful and thoughtful nods around the table.

"So," said Pagnell slowly, feeling his way through the concept, "the insurer is like a god."

"If you will," said Jynn.

"The people who want to protect their businesses or goods —"

"Or whatever you like."

"— make an offering to the insurer, as they would to a god?"

"As you say."

"Because although the insurer isn't a god, they have the wealth to pay reparations if the business or goods are destroyed. Because instead of holy power they've just got lots and lots of money."

"Correct."

There was a nervousness in Pagnell's expression and as he looked at Chrindle and Maegor, that nervousness spread.

"So, basically, you're saying — *you* are saying — that the wealthiest people in society can fulfil the same roles as gods?"

"In a manner of speaking."

"And in a manner of speaking you are. And, these wealthy people, offering this stand-in god service, are you one of them?"

"I might be," said Jynn with a modest shrug.

Pagnell moved his chair several feet further up the table from Jynn. On the other side of Jynn, Chrindle did likewise.

"What?" said Jynn, laughing.

Pagnell pointed up at the open sky. "I'm not sure how good Lekki's aim is."

"It's not sacrilege," Jynn argued. "It's just business."

"I'd check that out with a priest first," said Maegor.

Jynn sighed irritably. "It's supply and demand. I'm just meeting a need, going where the market forces take me.

Speaking of which, I've had some wealthy and influential friends complain to me last night." He gave Chrindle a firm stare. "Someone's been spreading rumours that dragons are attracted to gold."

"The wizard told us!" said Chrindle. "The master of dragons said."

"I said they like gold," said Pagnell.

"They were specifically drawn by its gravity, you said."

"Those were not the words."

"Whoever is to blame," said Jynn, "gold has suddenly lost its lustre, metaphorically at least. If the gold in your pocket increases your chances of being frazzle by dragonfire then people will be all the keener to use it to settle their debts and far less inclined to take it as payment, preferring silver or copper or other mediums of currency."

"Does it matter how people pay for things?" said Chrindle. "Money is money."

"Except when gold is losing its value. The gold in your strongbox isn't what it once was."

"It's shrinking?"

"So to speak."

"Thieves?"

"It's not thieves!"

Chrindle narrowed her eyes. "And these wealthy friends of yours, are they also in the god-faking insurance business like yourself?"

"What? Why?"

"They ape the gods and their treasure hoards start magically shrinking..."

"It's not the gods!" snapped Jynn.

"The gods do move in mysterious ways," said Maegor.

"Especially Pedlo," said Pagnell and mimed a little sideways waddle, complete with hands as crab claws.

"Have none of you even a basic grasp of economics?" said the much put-out lord treasurer.

"No, but none of us have had our gold cursed by the gods," said Chrindle smarmily.

7

In late afternoon, the mass of baked human effluent that plugged the River Turge caused the river to burst its banks. A lake of water, brown and soupy began to grow in the west of the city. The members of the privy council had an unparalleled view from their lofty hall.

"Someone needs to do something about that," said Cunnan.

"Let them bloody drown," muttered Jynn who had been in a sulk for much of the day.

"The garderobes in the castle would get blocked from time to time," said Maegor. "A good flushing with water would see them clear."

"I think its an excess of water that's the problem here," said Chrindle.

"Or a good poke with a long stick. The turding stick."

"Nice to know it has a name," said Pagnell.

"Wielded by the finest turdsmen in the castle."

Pagnell contemplated this.

"And there wouldn't happen to be a Union of Turdsmen we could get out there to shift that blockage?"

"It would hardly be a large union," said Maegor.

"Don't hold with garderobes myself," said Jynn.

"We don't have them aboard ship," agreed Cunnan.

Chrindle looked like she did not want to be drawn into a discussion of such a vulgar nature.

"Surely, wizard, you must know some spells."

"I do," agreed Pagnell heartily and then caught her meaning. "But not for matters such as this."

"Aye, one of your wizard bangs or poppers would make short work of that," said Cunnan.

"I don't think I have any 'bangs or poppers' as you put it."

"I thought that's what wizards were all about. Whizzes, bangs, fireballs."

"Looking all mysterious," said Jynn.

"Aye. Smoking pipes and turning up unexpected-like to declare new kings."

"Or take unsuspecting souls on quests," said Chrindle.

"Mixing potions in dusty towers."

"Meddling in the affairs of men."

"Reading spells from forbidden tomes."

"And calling down destruction on people what don't respect you."

"Well, I can assure you I don't do any of that," said Pagnell. "Except perhaps the meddling part."

The privy council were generally unimpressed.

"Are you sure you're a proper wizard?" said Jynn.

"He doesn't have a hat," said Maegor.

"And that's not much of a beard," said Chrindle.

"Neither of which are essential requirements," Pagnell said testily. "Of course I am a wizard, a proper wizard."

"And do you know any spells?"

"Several. But I have chosen to specialise. What good does it do if all the wizards of the north are fire and lightning weather mages?"

"Oh," said Cunnan. "And what's your specialism?"

Pagnell stood as straight and as tall as he could and tugged his coat into shape.

"Oral hygiene and innovative dentistry."

"What?" said Chrindle.

"You mean... teeth?" said Maegor.

"Exactly," said Pagnell and treated them all to a shining white smile. "Teeth are very important."

"Teeth?" said Jynn.

"What would we do if we had no teeth?"

"Eat soup," suggested Cunnan.

"From the health of the mouth, the health of the body extends," said Pagnell. "And I've devoted myself to the study and care of teeth. You can tell a lot about an individual by their teeth."

"Oh, well," said Maegor frivolously, "maybe you should inspect the thanes downstairs and decide which one should be the next king."

"Always happy to offer an opinion."

Cunnan leaned on the balcony. He did so gingerly. Much of the masonry in the city had been knocked loose by the dragon's fleeting visit and he didn't trust it to hold his weight entirely.

"Shame. A wizard with proper bangs and poppers could have shifted that blockage in no time."

"I'm sorry to disappoint," said Pagnell tartly. "Although I do have here..." He rummaged among the pouches and purses pinned to the inside of his coat before coming up with a spherical glass vial. "No. Perhaps too strong."

"What is it?" said Cunnan, looking at the white powder in the vial.

"Glasswort sudanum. An extract of my own devising. The Aumerian glassmakers use something similar as a flux. I find it has remarkable pain-relieving properties."

"We're neither making glass nor suffering with pains."

"True but it also has the unfortunate quality of reacting violently with water."

"How violently?"

"Very violently."

Jynn tucked his thumbs into his belt. "And what good will that do against the biggest turd Grome has every seen?"

"Tur— *effluent* is mostly water," said Pagnell.

"Remind me never to ask you for a cup of water."

Pagnell contemplated the vial. "As I say, it might be too powerful."

"We could go down and give it a try," said Chrindle. "It is our sworn duty to shift that mass of filth."

"I don't personally remember swearing that particular oath," said Cunnan but, even as he said it, was leaving the balcony and waving the wizard on to the long stairs.

8

J ynn and Maegor stayed on the balcony to watch.

"There they are," said Jynn soon enough.

Maegor squinted and saw that the man was right.

Three figure moved from the gates of the castle, along the ruined road to the edge of the sludgy lake that had formed across a portion of the city. Maegor could see figures leaning out of windows of buildings marooned in the rising waters, watching with similar interest.

It was still possible to approach the baked plug without getting one's feet wet. The river, unfortunately, had not managed to find its way back to its original course.

"So, the plan…" said Jynn.

"Is to cause some calamitous disruption to the solid mass so that the pressure of water behind it will flush it all away."

"Like giving cabbage soup to a constipated grandmother," nodded Jynn.

"My, what rich imagery you conjure, lord treasurer." Maegor coughed suddenly. "Is that another gold statue they're building?"

Jynn lazily looked downstream to where Maegor was looking. "The Temple of the Dragon is proving popular. And it doesn't hurt to advertise. And since, as I pointed out," he added grumpily, "gold is not what it used to be, it's become an increasingly cheap construction material. Oh, our master of horses is stepping out..."

Maegor looked back to the sewage dam.

Chrindle was indeed stepping out onto its hard dried surface.

"A crown says she falls in," said Jynn.

"I'm not betting on her life," said Maegor.

"You think she'll fall though?"

"No. She's far too nimble."

"A crown then."

Maegor bristled and then said, "A crown. A crown says she will be fine."

"You're on."

Below, Chrindle edged out onto the pie-crust, moving in a wide-legged scuttle. She made for the opening near its centre where the unfortunate fellow had fallen through the day before. She had something — the vial presumably — raised high in her hand.

Shouts drifted up, faint and wordless.

Chrindle lobbed the vial into the hole with force and then ran for her life. She appeared to be jamming her fingers in her ears as she did. Yards from the edge of the crust, the surface gave way, Chrindle sank in, fought furiously, lifted her feet out with sheer effort and stumbled desperately towards Pagnell and Cunnan who had taken shelter behind a tumbledown wall.

Maegor counted silently.

"Any moment…"

He paused, held off, expecting to be interrupted by an explosive shower of filth. And, even as he paused, it occurred to him only then that effluent was known to give off flammable marsh gas and perhaps the explosion would be even larger than the wizard had anticipated…

But nothing happened. Nothing occurred at all. No explosion, great or small. No pop. No fizzle. Nothing.

"Maybe we need to wait a little longer," said Jynn but without much hope.

Down on the street, three crouching figures stood up from behind their shelter. One waved its arms angrily at another and then all three trudged despondently back towards the castle.

"Wizards," Maegor muttered.

9

Maegor heard the footsteps on the stairs. Two sets of footsteps and the *schlup-schlup* of the third person. He judged the smell to have arrived marginally before the privy councillors themselves. Chrindle was painted up to her knees with a disturbing colour palette of various browns, ranging from a near yellow mustard colour, through shades that toyed with earthy and unearthly greens, to dark peaty tones that verged on black.

"Gods above us!" exclaimed Maegor. "Do you have to bring that stench in here?"

Chrindle said nothing, strode to the corner and trying to entirely avoid using her hands, wriggled, scraped and kicked until she was able to fling away first one boot and then the other. Each landed with a squelch. Castle drudgeons appeared to remove the offending items.

"See that they're cleaned!" Chrindle shouted after them. "And bring me a tub of hot water!"

Drudgeons bobbed their heads and fled.

"What happened?" said Jynn. "Where were the pops and bangs?"

"We were promised violent disruptions," said Maegor.

There was a very tight expression on Pagnell's face.

"Someone," he said, evidently trying to keep calm. "Forgot to unstopper the vial before throwing it."

"Someone," said Chrindle, not bothering to keep her cool, "didn't tell me that I had to!"

"I shouted. Stopper! Stopper!"

"I thought you were shouting, 'Stop her! Stop her!'"

"Why would I be shouting that?"

"Maybe you had lost your nerve!" snapped Chrindle as she delicately stripped off her slimed and sodden trews. "I don't know what wizards shout or why!"

"So that's it?" said Jynn. "You haven't got another bottle of the stuff?"

"It would take a ton of glasswort and a month of my time to make some more," said Pagnell bitterly. "Our best hope is that the sludge rots through the cork stopper eventually."

Chrindle made the mistake of experimentally sniffing at her removed garments and gagged in response.

"Eventually?" said Cunnan.

Pagnell sighed. "Probably never."

"Well, maybe," said Jynn, "we ought to adjourn for today. One great plan has come to nowt, the master of horses is stinking the room out and I'm sure we've all got better things to do."

"We have business to attend to here," said Maegor.

"And if I have to haul my arse up those stairs twice in one

day," said Cunnan, "then I expect to have done it for a good reason."

Jynn fanned in front of his nose.

"Could we not meet somewhere else temporarily?"

"Or somewhere else permanently?" said Cunnan. "Nearer ground level perhaps."

"There are traditions to be respected," said Maegor. "The privy council traditionally met in the South Tower but that is in no fit state to accommodate since the dragon made its roost there but in the reign of King — I forget his name, somebody-or-other — this hall was used."

"Really?" said Pagnell.

"I'm fairly sure. I read it in one of the histories."

"No, I meant about the dragon in the South Tower. I searched there and found no sign."

"Searched?" said Cunnan.

Pagnell gave him a frank look. "Yes. I am looking for any... *leavings* from the dragon. Skin, hide, claws. They all have useful properties. I am particularly keen to lay my hands on some dragon eggshell, even a small quantity."

"Oh, he has dark plans," said Jynn.

"Hardly," said Pagnell.

Barefoot and stinking to high heaven, Chrindle dragged one of the chairs from the table over to the fireplace.

"What's it for then?" she said, once she had finished scraping. "The eggshell."

"Toothpaste," said Pagnell.

"Pardon?" said Maegor.

"Toothpaste."

"A spell that turns your teeth to paste," said Jynn. "Dark sorcery."

"A paste to keep your teeth clean," said Pagnell and grinned broadly so everyone could see his unnaturally white gnashers. "A polish. From one whole dragon egg, I could produce enough to clean every tooth in this city for ten years, but I've only been able to harvest fragments before and I nearly died in the attempt."

Servants came up the stairs with a steaming and soapy half-barrel of water. Chrindle clicked her fingers and indicated they should put it before her chair by the fire. Another servant had brought bowls of petals with her, in the wildly optimistic hope of masking the stink in the room. Two more came with food and drink.

"Did you try to steal the shell from an actual dragon?" said Cunnan.

"No," said Pagnell, lifting a flagon of beer from the servant's tray as she passed. "I was faced with a far more insidious foe. In a place that smelled almost as bad as this very hall."

10

STRANGOL

In my defence [said Pagnell] I would point out that the village had appeared destroyed. Or at least abandoned.

A stench hung over the place. A midden heap of fish heads was the thought that leaped initially to mind. But there was an undercurrent of pervasive filth, of a people who had embraced a lifestyle so base that everyone wanted their own midden heap of fish heads to improve the smell.

I was not quite at the end of the world, just the scrappy leftover bits of the world that nobody wanted. It was bleak up there, with grey rocks jutting out of an equally grey sea under a sky that bulged with rain. The land was mostly scrub, brambles and moss, interspersed with treacherous marshes. The trees were spindly, desperate things. It was the kind of place that offered little opportunity to a wizard, a dentist or a roving diplomat-for-hire and I could present myself as any of the three if the situation required.

The situation did not require it.

The villagers caught me in the act of levering two beautiful pieces of dragon shell from the carved pole at the centre of the village. The situation required fast legs and the agility of a hare and I possessed neither. The people's garments were fashioned from rancid hide, tied on with lengths of twine. Their faces were barely discernible underneath foul beards which hung in matted strings down their chests. Their red-rimmed eyes blinked constantly, as though they hadn't slept in weeks and the grey light of day hurt them.

"A stranger, Knubbig!" yelled one in the Uvås language, revealing a mouth full of rotten teeth that made my dentist's heart give an involuntary leap.

"It is, Snöflinga!" declared a bulky man.

I had clearly turned into the most interesting thing these unfortunates had seen in a long while so I pushed back my hood. No sense in hiding my handsome face from these onlookers. A collective gasp arose. I get that a lot. It's the burden I bear, being possessed of such good looks. And soap.

"I didn't want to cause any alarm. I can see that you're a tight-knit community, and I realise that the appearance of a stranger could be disruptive. But now that I have your attention, I would like to talk to you about the wonders of oral hygiene and innovative dentistry."

In truth, my command of Uvås isn't that great and so what I actually said was 'the wonders of mouth-washing and cunning tooth-trickery' but it was good enough. I bowed low, sweeping the dragon shell pieces behind my back and out of view.

"Let us be strangers no more," I said smoothly. "I am

Newport Pagnell, friend to all, valued advisor to the Yarwish king, the guildmasters of Aumeria and —"

"'E's nicked Storfeten's eyes," came a squeaky voice from behind.

I turned to see a thing that might have been a child or might have been the unholy offspring of a very lonely man and something he met in a cave. Its grubby finger was pointed directly at my clasped hands. Knubbig's strong hands prised mine apart. Out came the fragments of dragon shell.

"Thief!" yelled Snöflinga.

"Kill him!" yelled another.

"Take him to Bredskär!" came a cry.

I was suddenly shoved towards the large hall and through the rent in the wall that passed for a door.

"Bredskär, you old goat!" yelled Knubbig. These people liked yelling. It seemed the only way of getting a response from each other.

"I arise," croaked a voice, "from a night in pitched battle with Strangol."

In the gloom, a shadow shifted with much moaning. The crone was bent low, so that her matted hair dragged on the ground. She wore robes that gave her an authoritative and mystical air. I mean, they weren't anything like mine. Even after several weeks of travel-wear, mine were still clearly the robes of an up-and-coming sorcerer of note and perhaps one of the leading proponents in the art of dentistry but hers were in such filthy disrepair that they looked much as if she'd lived in them, slept in them, perhaps even been recently disinterred from an ancient grave in them.

Her gait was that of someone crossing a storm-tossed ship. She lurched towards us in a zigzag fashion, unsure where exactly we were. I'm not even confident that she knew where the floor was, as she seemed to miss her footing several times.

"We have caught a thief," said Knubbig.

"Are we not all thieves?" mumbled Bredskär. "And is not time the greatest thief of all?"

"Yes," said Knubbig, "but this man has actually stolen something."

Bredskär's gaze travelled across the group and caused several faces to flush with guilt. I wondered whether this was a technique to unnerve her followers, or whether she was just having trouble focusing.

I coughed. "Just a simple misunderstanding. I'm sure we can clear this up. I came here to study the customs of your people, and naturally I wanted a closer look at your most sacred, um, pole. I'm afraid to say that it's in such a state of disrepair that the pieces fell into my hands. But I do have about myself some dental fixative and, I'm sure that —"

Bredskär spluttered with something like laughter, punctuated with an immense belch.

"Better out than in," she proclaimed.

"Yes," I nodded, not wishing to cause further offence. For some reason this caused much hilarity. All of the other men reacted as if they'd been given an instruction. They converged on me, lifted me above their heads and marched out, chanting, "Better out than in."

"Wait!" I yelled.

"Better out than in!"

"Wait! What does it mean?"

A mouth pressed close to my ear. I recognised the voice of Knubbig. "Better out than in. We love it! You might not, I suppose. We nail your guts to the post of Storfeten, and then we make you walk around it until you've unwound all of them."

I craned my head and saw the one called Snöflinga already standing by the pole with a mallet and a bunch of wickedly long nails in one hand and a large fish hook in the other. The pile of rotten offal at the base of the pole made sense now.

"But why?" I cried. "Why?"

It's a right laugh," said Knubbig amiably. "Sometimes it goes on all evening before death comes."

We stopped at the pole and they dumped me on the ground.

I cast about for an escape route.

"Don't do this," I said.

"But we want to," said Knubbig.

"I have a letter of safe passage from the king in Yarwich who demands that all subjects offer no hindrance to —"

The paper in my hand was first ripped away and then ripped up.

"I could offer my dental services for free! Half price at least! You, sir, look like you'd appreciate a set of dentures."

Some of the more eager villagers were already pulling at my clothes to get to my belly and my guts. I never realised how attached to my guts I was until that moment.

"Killing me will make a terrible mess," I said lamely.

"We're used to mess," said Knubbig. "See what Strangol

does to our village day in and day out." He waved an arm at the ruined village around them. "We bear it with great fortitude and take any spot of relief from the misery we can get. Killing you will make us happy."

"But will it?" I asked deeply.

"Oh, yes," said Knubbig, "We've not been able to do 'better out than in' for ages."

I shuddered as grubby little digits pulled open my robes and exposed my stomach. Snöflinga came in with his fish hook.

"Wait!" I squealed. "I am well-versed in the ways of Strangol. I could help rid you of Strangol forever!"

"Could you?" said Knubbig.

"Yes," I said, this of course being a complete lie. I had never heard of Strangol before. I didn't know if it was a man or a beast or a tribe of marauding grimlocks.

Knubbig laughed. "Defeat Strangol? Strangol has made fools of us for years. It brings sickness and destroys our livelihoods." There were grumbles of agreement from the tribe. "Our wives and foodstores never last long because of the scourge that is Strangol."

"And I could put an end to that," I suggested. The point of Snöflinga's hook rested against my delicate bellyflesh.

"Only a salt-witch could magic away the hell of Strangol," he said.

"And do you gut salt-witches?" I asked.

"No."

"Then in that case, I am —"

"We burn them alive and scatter their ashes into the sea."

"I am not a salt-witch," I continued with barely a stumble, "but I do possess the power to defeat Strangol."

Knubbig scoffed. The others scoffed too. There was a lot of general scoffing.

"To think that an unbearded man could stop Strangol is absurd!"

"I have a beard."

"Barely any sort of beard."

"I can help you all!" I told the crowd. "Strangol can be defeated. I am your only chance. In fact, you may never get another opportunity like this. Are you prepared to pass that by? Are you?"

There was a palpable sense of frustration. Snöflinga, eager to get busy with the disembowelling, scowled at the group's hesitation.

"He can't control Strangol. No-one can!"

The shaman, Bredskär, threw up her hands, nearly falling out of the grip of her helpers. "We will let the sea maidens decide!"

There was a surge of mumbling, sounding surprised and not a little outraged. I wondered whether guests were not normally permitted to see the sea maidens. Perhaps they were beautiful. I smiled. I have some considerable experience at charming beautiful maidens. I wrote a small treatise on it once.

They grunted and tried to lift me again.

"Stop that!" I snapped. "I am capable of walking."

They looked a little sullen and disappointed, but off we set towards the shore.

Bredskär, supported on both sides, led the way to a rocky

promontory. One of her helpers nudged her awake. She took a moment to register her surroundings. She turned and saw me, which I think jogged her memory. She cleared her throat and then started to make a horrific noise. I have heard it said that some mountain dwellers practise a form of primitive ululation in order to be heard across a valley, but this was so piercing and discordant that I felt sure it was part of my punishment for stealing the dragon shell. Rather than covering their ears, the other members of the tribe joined in. The air was filled with the sound of grown men and women making a noise like a pack of wolves with a severe digestive complaint. This carried on to the point at which I was ready to go back to the original plan and perhaps offer to nail my own guts to the post when silence fell. Bredskär raised her arms to the sea.

"Behold! The maidens approach!"

I looked. A fat and hairy seal heaved out of the waves and plopped onto a rock a few feet in front of us. One of the villagers threw it a fish head which it caught expertly and gulped down. Moments later there were another three seals on the rock.

"Sea maidens, huh?" I said.

"The divine handmaidens of Storfeten," said Knubbig.

By the Eastern Sea, sailors tell tales of mermaids and I have always fancied that those tales are nothing more than drunken sailors seeing distant seals, perhaps with strands of seaweed draped artfully over their heads. Beer and loneliness will make a man see any number of things that aren't there. But, I have to say, a sailor would have to drink a hell of a lot of beer to think these blubbery sacks were anything other than the ugly cows of the deep.

"Salt-witch or not witch the sea maidens will say which," said Bredskär.

I watched Bredskär listening carefully to the honking of the seals (who were surely expressing a desire for more fish heads) and I realised that my life depended on these seals. One old corpulent sow looked at me and made a low blarting noise. Bredskär gasped and nodded, her hands together in reverence.

"The maidens have spoken," she said.

"Yes?" I said.

"We must accommodate our guest and listen to his advice."

The shaman looked exhausted by all the excitement and her head sagged forward. The journey back was accompanied by the sound of her snoring, with the occasional loud fart.

"Tell me more about Strangol," I said.

"But you said you knew everything," said Snöflinga suspiciously.

"I do," I said emphatically. "But I need to know what you know. To build a castle on the swamp of your ignorance, I need to know how deep that swamp is."

"That's profound," said Knubbig. "Is that ancient wisdom?"

"No, it's my wisdom, which is better because it's fresh and

hasn't had time to go stale. Tell me, when does Strangol attack?"

The men of the tribe looked at each other and then at me.

"Depends?" ventured one and the others nodded readily.

"Yeah, it depends," they said.

"Night, usually," said Knubbig.

"Good," I said. "That's something. And where does the attack come from? What direction?"

The clueless men stared at each other again and then at me.

"It can hit you from any direction," said Snöflinga.

"And no direction at all," added another.

They were idiots. I had allowed myself to be captured by idiots with pointy sticks.

"Does that help?" asked Knubbig.

"It does," I said. "The swamp is deep. I'm amazed you've survived against Strangol for so long."

With minds as dull as these, I was surprised they hadn't all swallowed their own tongues or accidentally drowned themselves already.

I organised them into work groups at once.

"Snöflinga, you're in charge of the ditch digging team. Knubbig, you'll be leading the construction crew. Let's walk the perimeter."

The group followed me as I paced out the route for the semi-circular defensive ditch that they'd need to defend themselves from any hostile invader. The digging team set to work while I discussed some designs with Knubbig and a couple of the brighter looking men.

"You'll make a wall inside the ditch to guard the perimeter," I explained. "Timber will be best for that, but if we can't find enough, you can use the mud bricks you've employed for your buildings. What I'm going to show you now is the design for a weapon that you can use against Strangol."

"A weapon?" they gasped as one.

"Yes. This knowledge is prized and you must take great care never to reveal what you know outside of this tribe. Also, you need to take care that the weapon itself does not fall into the hands of your enemy. Understand?"

They all nodded, their eyes wide.

I showed them, with the aid of some diagrams scratched in the dirt and a small demonstration with a bendy twig, how a military assault catapult might be constructed from timber, using a counterweight made from a sealskin sack filled with stones. It turned out that Knubbig had an engineer's eye and he made several suggestions for materials to use (mostly seal-based) and improvements to the design. They got to work while I took on the time-honoured role of supervisor, strolling from team to team and shouting out instructions. The clouds had cleared in the late afternoon and my mood was optimistic. The ditch-digging team finished more quickly than I had envisaged, so I put them to work on the defensive wall, and by evening of that day the camp was transformed. There was a ditch around the entire circuit, with drawbridges for daytime convenience. In pride of place, next to the hall, was their newly constructed catapult siege engine. It was ready for a test firing in the morning, we would simply wheel it down to the rocks, fill the launch cup and pull out the pin that held the counterweight into position.

As I sat and watched the last dying rays of the sun, Knubbig walked over.

"You are watching the sea maidens," he said.

"Yes," I lied. I was, in truth, preparing what few spells I had that might be used in pitched battle. If Strangol did attack the village tonight, Newport Pagnell wasn't going to rely on moronic seal-worshippers for protection.

"Tonight, they swim to the land of Storfeten to speak with the gods."

He waved a hand at the evening stars that were just coming out.

"See here? This is Gurkört, the elder."

I looked at the vague splatter of stars he was indication. I nodded in a way that I hope conveyed politeness, but a lack of interest in further demonstrations.

"Look!" he said. "That one is Snitta, the dreamer, and next to her is Mumsig the perverse."

"And all the gods are... seals?"

"Seals are made in their image, as close to divine perfection as is possible. There. That one is Ljuvlig the Desirable."

As I followed Knubbig's arm across the sky, I realised that it was pretty handy to have seals as your gods. Any random cluster of stars could be called upon to represent a seal, being as shapeless an animal as it's possible to imagine.

. . .

WE WALKED to Bredskär's hall. There was to be a feast in honour of all that we'd achieved. In the foetid, tumbledown slum, I took my place at the head of the table, next to Bredskär. She snoozed in her chair. I think she might have been tied into an upright position.

"The sea maidens are everything to us," said Knubbig, sitting down. "They give us food, drink and everything that we need."

He poured liquid into a tankard and passed it to me.

I looked at it.

"Everything?"

"Everything."

I took a swig and gagged. It was like rancid fish guts mixed with sour milk. "What is this, um, stuff?"

"It's fiskö. Potent, eh? Stronger than your foreign beer," sneered Knubbig. "It is a great delicacy that we enjoy on special occasions, like the going down of the sun."

"I can't drink this."

Knubbig looked at me sadly. "To refuse fiskö is to dishonour the Storfeten. We would hate to kill you after the help you have given us, but it would be necessary. Drink up. It gets much better after the first five cups."

I faked a big swig. I would find a way to tip it away later.

"So, how do you make fiskö?" I asked.

He sniggered at my foolishness. "First we must collect the milk."

"Seal milk?"

"What else?"

"And seals are happy to let you do this?" I asked.

"It's all part of the intimate relationship we have with the sea maidens."

"Oh?"

"Every boy must milk his first seal to reach manhood," said Knubbig.

"And by milk his first seal, you mean...?" I had to ask.

"I mean milk the seal," said Knubbig, rolling his eyes. "Then he may lie with her, of course."

"Of course."

I was rescued from this avenue of conversation by a swelling of voices. The tankards swung and slopped their foul contents as the tribe started to sing. Bredskär woke up at this point and led the singing. It was a song that featured many obscure words from the local dialect, but as far as I could make out it was the tale of the coming of Storfeten, the seal goddess who watched over the village. At the end of every verse (and there were many) the entire group drained their tankard to the bottom. There was just enough time as someone took up the next verse to pass the jugs around the tables and top up all of the tankards. I still hadn't drunk any of the fiskö. I had surreptitiously topped up Bredskär's tankard from mine when she slept, I had poured some onto the floor down the side of the table, and I had even filled my boots. I felt was going to regret tainting my boots in such a way, but I was running out of places to put it. I looked around me and realised that it no longer mattered how careful I was to dispose of the stuff. As fast as they could top up their tankards and pour it down their necks, they were also spilling it on every surrounding surface as they sang, cackled with laughter and leaned over to hug each other in drunken camaraderie. The place was awash with fiskö. It ran across the tables and puddled on the floor. If I hadn't already filled my boots it would undoubtedly be filling them up anyway. The room stank like a fishmonger's cast offs.

I glanced across at Bredskär who I realised had been drunk all day long. I found it miraculous that she was able to function in any way, given the evident power of the drink. She grinned at me (oh, look at those gums, I thought, I could have fashioned her a lovely set of false gnashers) held her tankard aloft and then passed once more into unconsciousness, her head sagging on her chest. I decided that I might follow her sterling example, so I discreetly moved back from the table and went to find myself a quiet corner. And by 'quiet corner', I meant somewhere that didn't reek of the bad end of a seal where I might be safe for a few minutes, if and when the mysterious Strangol attacked.

I wedged myself between two rocks near the defensive trench down by the shore and wrapped my cloak around me. I managed to get an hour or two's sleep before I was woken by the unmistakeable sounds of a violent incursion. There was shouting coming from all around me, and the grunting and smashing of an unseen enemy.

"Strangol."

I hesitated. I had agreed to help these morons, but I had no intention of joining any fighting. I have always relied on my wits for survival, along with my modest spellcasting abilities. When it comes to confrontation, my skills have always leaned towards hiding and running away. These are good skills and I have known many a fine warrior who could have survived if he'd taken advantage of them. I got up to have a look. It was deepest night but I could see what was happening. This was partly because the moon was bright. And partly because the main hall was on fire.

I kept a careful eye out for Strangol. I still wasn't certain whether it was a monstrous beast or a multitude of grimlocks. Detail had been sparse.

Knubbig ran past, his face contorted with horror. I grabbed his arm.

"What is it?"

"Strangol!" he howled.

"Shush now," I pleaded. "Calm yourself. Is the danger gone? Can we organise a chain of people to throw water on the fire?"

"You don't know what you're dealing with!" he yelled drunkenly and ran off. To my astonishment, he ran to the fire, pulled off a burning plank and waved it above his head with a blood-curdling roar. Then he came over and touched the flaming timber to the hut behind me. The flames licked up the outside and into the thatch. He cackled with momentary glee, but then a tribesman appeared and struck him over the back of the head with an empty barrel, sending him sprawling into the dirt.

"I was to have that hut!" he yelled. "You knew I wanted it!"

"I know!" shouted Knubbig, getting shakily to his feet. "I did this for you! So it didn't fall into enemy hands!"

"You fool!" howled the other.

"Enemy hands!" burbled Knubbig.

"I should have been the one to set fire to it! How can you be so selfish?"

They sprang at each other and battered wildly. Arms and legs were flying everywhere, as their fighting abilities were compromised by their extreme drunkenness. But why were they fighting when Strangol was upon them?

I ran towards the flaming meeting hall. In the light of the inferno, I could see carnage and destruction all around. Men and women struggled as silhouettes against the flames. But the only thing they seemed to be struggling with was each other or themselves. There was no sign of Strangol or the Strangol or the Strangols, whatever they were.

I pulled Snöflinga off a poor man he was attempting to throttle with his own beard.

"Stop it, man! Are you bewitched?"

"Are you trying to steal my kittens?" warbled Snöflinga.

"That doesn't even make sense!" I shouted.

"You don't make sense!" he slurred. "What are you? A man or a... or a..." His line of thought, which he was clearly struggling with anyway, seemed to have wandered away completely. "A man or a different man? Hmmm? Eh?"

The man was sozzled. It occurred to me that I had the advantage over every person in the camp, simply by being sober and co-ordinated. I climbed up onto the base of the catapult we had built and held up my hands.

"Can everyone just calm down?" I called out. They ignored me. I might as well have shouted into a hurricane.

I reluctantly dipped into my repertoire and cast Voltan's Magnificent Voice.

"EVERYBODY! STOP WHAT YOU'RE DOING AT ONCE!"

That did it. Stinking seal-lovers and their hideous fishwives stopped choking each other, bashing holes in their own homes and generally setting fire to anything that wasn't too damp to burn. Snöflinga and his wrestling partner stumbled apart, panting with exhaustion and unfocused rage.

"WHAT ARE YOU ALL DOING?" I demanded.

"He was going to steal my best boat!" shouted out a drunkard with a smashed oar in his hand.

"She was giving my dog a funny look!" added another.

"He's got posh trousers and he knows it!" added a third. And then there was a tumult of cries.

"People are jealous of my hut!"

"He's been kissing my wife!"

"For the last time, I'm not your wife!"

"I'm not happy with who I am! You know, on the inside!"

"SILENCE!" I commanded. "HOW CAN YOU HOPE TO FACE STRANGOL WHEN YOU ARE LIKE THIS?"

In the light of many fires, dozens of eyes blinked. I am a clever man but I don't always work things out as quickly as I would like.

"THIS IS STRANGOL, ISN'T IT?" I said. "THIS DRUNKEN FRENZY."

An entire village nodded sheepishly.

"IT'S STUPID."

They nodded some more, their chins disappearing into their beards.

"AND DO YOU THINK YOU COULD JUST STOP IT AND CALM DOWN?"

Knubbig looked at me sideways and mumbled, "s'pose."

"No!" cried Bredskär, careering towards me, wearing a

headpiece that mimicked the head and shoulders of a seal. As she drew nearer, I saw with horror that it *was* the head and shoulders of a seal, which had somehow been hollowed out into a fleshy, stinking face mask.

She clambered unsteadily onto the catapult beside me and pointed an accusing finger at them all, swivelling to glare at each and every one of them.

"Strangol has fled while moon's still up?" she slurred. "How can this be?"

"We've just sort of stopped," said Knubbig. "You know, cos it's stupid."

Bredskär was having none of it. "Only witchcraft can explain such a thing! Salt-witch!" she screeched and pointed her accusing finger at me.

"IT'S NOT WITCHCRA –" I cancelled my spell with a wave. "It's not witchcraft," I said. "These men have simply woken to the foolishness of their actions."

"That is *exactly* what a salt-witch would say!" she screeched.

I may have rolled my eyes at that point, which didn't help.

"Storfeten demands we drink fiskö," she screeched. "Fiskö brings Strangol. Strangol is sacred!"

"But we smash our things up and upset everyone," said Knubbig. "We could just... not do it, maybe?"

"Heresy! You must atone for that immediately. Go and break something! Yes, now! You first and then the rest of you can kill the salt-witch. That should get the party going again."

Knubbig picked up a hammer from the wreckage that surrounded us and cast about for something to smash. His heart was clearly not in it. He came over to the catapult, which saddened me slightly. I'd been rather proud of it.

"Do it!" yelled Bredskär. "Appease the gods!"

Two things happened pretty much simultaneously. One was that I realised Bredskär wasn't just standing on the catapult base like me but had stepped into the cup to place herself above me. The other thing was Knubbig's hammer whacking the retaining pin from the launch mechanism.

Bredskär was flung high into the sky towards the sea. I was the only one sufficiently sober to register what had happened. The rest of the tribe just looked confused at Bredskär's sudden disappearance, blinking and looking around to see if she was hiding.

"Where's she gone?"

"Magic!"

"Salt-witch!"

"Ah," I said and prepared to run like never before when I saw that, rather than racing to seize me, they were cowering before me. Knubbig was unwillingly thrust forward to speak to me.

"Mighty salt-witch. Please don't be angry with us." He wrung his hands together pitifully.

"Look, I'm not a —" I sighed. "Fine. Yes. I'm a salt-witch. And I'm angry."

"It was Bredskär!" said Snöflinga. "She did it."

"And look what happened to her," I said pointedly. I'm not usually one for flinging pickled old women into the sea but now it had occurred I was going to exploit it.

"How can we make amends?" pleaded Knubbig.

"Well..."

I looked towards the sacred pole and the pieces of dragon shell that had been inexpertly put back in place.

I was gone before dawn, heading towards the marshy hinterland as quickly as possible, as though idiocy was contagious and I didn't want to catch it. As I hurried off, I fancied I could hear the sound of sorrow-drowning fiskö being poured into tankards.

"Y̶ou made that up," said Maegor.

"I did not," said Pagnell. "On my word of honour."

The five of them sat around the fire, Chrindle with her feet in the tub of still steaming water. The smell she had brought in which her had not gone but it had diffused and spread, become diluted until it was more of a background honk, rather than a direct assault on the nose. Having most of the roof missing and the wind blowing through must have helped.

"When we met you in here two days ago..." said Maegor.

Pagnell raised an eyebrow.

"You said you were a new appointment to the privy council," said Maegor.

"You *assumed* I was a new appointment to the council."

"I assumed you were a cleaner."

"I should have carried a broom with me."

"So, who are you?" said Cunnan, worrying at an apple from his plate.

"A dentist, a wizard."

"But who sent you?"

"No one. I'm a wizard. I just turned up, unexpected like."

"See?" said the lord admiral. "I told you that was what wizards were meant to be like."

"Come looking for dragon eggs," said Jynn.

"That too," said Pagnell.

Jynn stretched, picked his flagon of beer off the short table before him and inspected the dregs.

"So, Mr Wizard, which of the thanes downstairs do you think should be made king?"

"That's not for us to decide," said Chrindle.

"Not us, no," said Jynn. "We are but humble servants. But he's not even one of us. He's a foreigner to boot, aren't you?"

"Depends who you ask," said Pagnell. "And where."

"But you've seen them all."

"From afar. Bickering mostly."

"Maybe you should take a look at their teeth," said Chrindle. "Can a tooth-mage predict a man's future from his teeth?"

"Only if he's ever likely to enjoy tough steak again," said Pagnell. "They've all got fair claims on the throne. They've been keen to point out each other's suitability for the role ever since the dragon left. But, of course, they've all been keen to sing their own praises sufficiently that when the next king fails – as anyone who has to restore the kingdom after a dragon will fail — that they are the second best option in the land. No one truly wants to be the king but to be power behind the throne..."

"But who?" said Jynn.

Pagnell sighed. "Aegis the Short has the strongest blood claim to the throne but being related to the last mad king or the mad dragon queen who deposed him is probably not a good selling point. Waldau the One-Handed is certainly the most experienced warrior of them all but great warriors do not make great kings... Red Salka is a fierce woman and she spoke out against the dragon queen from the start but I suspect her reign would start with the settling of some old scores..."

"So who then, man?" said Cunnan.

"No one," said Pagnell. "None of them at least. You want my opinion?"

"I believe we asked for it," said Jynn testily.

"Stick a dummy on the throne and put a crown its head."

"I beg your pardon," said Maegor.

"Put a dummy, a guy, an empty shell on that throne. Let it wear the crown. The crown is round and meaningless, like a zero in mathematics, but just as important. The king's head is nothing but a place to store it. Put the crown on a dummy and let the privy council get on with the business of ruling. If it's worked for the last few days, it can work for a few months, maybe even years."

They all stared into the fire and gave it some thought.

"If we do that, would that be treason?" said Chrindle slowly.

"I don't know," said Cunnan equally slowly.

Jynn raised himself up out of his slouch and tapped Maegor with his fingertips.

"You owe me a crown," he said.

"We owe...?" said Maegor, startled. "The crown?"

"A crown," said Jynn and pointed at Chrindle. "Our wager. The master of horses here fell in."

Maegor shook his head.

"That's not falling in, lord treasurer. She barely got her feet wet."

"In is in, master of seals, and don't pretend otherwise."

"I wagered a crown that she would be fine."

Jynn wafted his hand in front of his nose. "You call that fine? Her boots will never be the same again."

Chrindle stood and struck an indignant pose. It would have looked far more effective if she hadn't done it in a knee-high tub of water.

"You two were betting on my life?"

"Just thought we'd make it interesting," said Jynn.

"Me risking my neck in service of the city wasn't interesting enough?"

Jynn shrugged. "Death is common here. Common and dull. But money, money is always interesting."

Maegor passed him a crown coin to shut him up.

C hrindle walked to the castle shortly after dawn. She had chambers in the castle as befitted her station but, as master of horses and lord commander of the city watch, she preferred to spend most of her nights down in the barracks in the city. Red cloaks told her it was an honour to have her lodge with them although she suspected that this wasn't true and that they'd rather have their commander stay at some distance. However, like it or not, she was sure they respected her for it and she made a point of being up and out with the earliest patrols of the day.

Her route from the north barracks to the castle required some small detour in order to avoid the shallow but growing lake that had formed around the River Turge. The waters met with the ash that still filled the streets and formed a grey pasty sludge. Charcoal collectors splashed about in their efforts to gather blackened wood from incinerated houses nearest the lake. Temple acolytes in the various colour-coded robes of their respective gods, walked around with buckets and carts, scooping up ash and bone and trying to look all holy and dignified while they did it.

"Excuse me, are you protected?"

Chrindle gave a small start. A little man with a nasal voice had somehow materialised at her elbow. He wore priestly robes that weren't exactly golden but had golden thread sewn through them in sufficient quantity to provide a general impression.

"What?" she said.

"Protected? Are you protected?"

Chrindle drew an inch of her sword blade, hoping that would make the point.

"Oh, no," the little man burst out laughing. "Oh, that is funny. No, I didn't mean that. That is priceless, my lady." He sighed as though utterly overcome with mirth. "Not 'protected'; protected."

"It is too early in the morning to put up with gibbering nonsense," she said. "Now, I must be about my business."

"Oh, I know," said the little man. "Important role in the castle. Mistress of horses —"

"Master of horses."

"I stand corrected, indeed I do. Master of horses. Apologies, my lady — my lord? — And what an important job, a dangerous job. Which is why I ask if you have protection."

Chrindle's hand twitched on the pommel of her sword. She didn't want to set the poor mad chap into further paroxysms of laughter and she feared that if she did she would be tempted to use the sword on him.

"At Dragon Mutual Assurance (a subsidiary of the Temple of Dragon)," he added in a quick, quiet tone, "we know that life has ups and downs and that all those little 'it'll never happens' happen all too often."

"What are you talking about?"

"Life insurance, my lady."

"Life insurance?"

"Exactly that. You are a sharp one, my lady. I knew you'd understand."

Chrindle had had enough, turned about and marched on then, seeing she was about the marching into the Turge lake, took a sharp left and marched that way in step. The little man from the Temple of the Dragon scurried to keep up with her.

"For just a small weekly premium, we can insure yourself and all your worldly belongings from harm."

"You guarantee I won't be harmed?"

"Or we pay appropriate compensation. Say if you were to lose that sword — and it's a beautiful sword, isn't it? — then we would buy you another one."

"Why would I lose my sword?"

"Who knows?" said the man enthusiastically. "It might be stolen."

"The commander of the red cloaks have her sword stolen?"

"How mortifying that would be. And all the red cloaks would be running around looking for it, tooting their whistles —"

"Red cloaks don't have whistles."

"Don't they? But the song..."

"Entirely inaccurate."

"Oh. And your sword has vanished without a trace then —"

"It would never be stolen."

"Then dropped in the river."

"Have people been talking?"

"Or melted by dragon fire."

"Along with the rest of me?"

"Ah, but we insure your life also. Dragon-related losses are our speciality."

Chrindle slowed, confused. "You'd pay for a replacement *me*?"

"Ah, sadly, not within our remit as of yet but we would make a very generous pay-out to your loved ones. We can also, with our executive package, arrange for prayers to be said for your soul (mortal or immortal, beliefs may vary, please read the small print)," he said in his weird quick voice. "We can ensure you have the best chance of favourable outcome post-mortem."

"This is nonsense, isn't it?" she said.

"It's the future, my lady. The two are often indistinguishable."

She put on a fresh turn of speed and walked fast enough to soon leave the little insurance salesman far behind.

"I'll send you one of our brochures, my lady," he called faintly after her.

She crossed the tiny trickle that was the downstream end of the River Turge. She took the wooden bridge by the Temple of the Dragon, not that the bridge was necessary any more. Pedestrians crossed the river bed easily and even local buildings were starting to expand out into the freed up space.

She entered the castle, climbed to the meeting hall and found the privy council already in session, the four councillors gathered around a set of weighing scales while a rather miffed priest of Buqit looked on.

"For one thing, it's wet," said Maegor.

"And?" said the priest.

"It stands to reason that wet ash is heavier than dry ash."

"Does it?" said the priest stiffly. "I wouldn't know about such things. There is a time for all things but I am unaware of when it would be time for a priest to compare wet ash with dry."

"It's flaming obvious, man," said Cunnan and dug his hand into the bucket. "Wet ash weighs more and since you're being paid for the disposal of the dead by the tonne we'd rather the ash you're disposing off was dry!"

"And yet... and yet..." said the priest in the airy tones of one who was about to go off into flights of whimsy, "it is curious that a bucket full of dry ash contains as much actual ash as a bucket full of ash and water."

"Curious how?" said Maegor, nonplussed.

"That the bucket, so perfect a metaphor for the human individual, is composed entirely of the physicality of human existence, the meat and bones as it were and yet — and yet! — has room for the water, the divine essence that too fills us all, the immortal spirit if you will."

"I don't see the relevance," said Maegor.

"Don't you see? Here we are quibbling over the weight of

a quantity of water. Are we not quibbling over the weight, the valuable weight, of the human soul?"

Everyone thought about this for a moment.

"No," said Cunnan. "No, we're bloody not, you daft apeth."

"But who can say what weight, what heft the soul takes on after death?"

"This man," said Meagor and indicated Pagnell the wizard. "He's done his experiments."

"I have," said Pagnell.

"With his burnt sausage."

"I did."

"That reminds me," said Cunnan, "I heard a song in the tavern last —"

"In fact, I am worried about the quality of these ashes," said Pagnell, cutting off Cunnan's recollection of what he'd heard the night before. "I'm not sure if these are human ashes at all."

"Of course they are," said the priest of Buqit. "Look. There's a finger."

"Artfully placed," Pagnell agreed. "But these have the general look of wood ash, possibly even paper."

"You can tell?"

"I can tell," said Pagnell. "Not only will you need to make sure the ashes are dry but that they are human."

"But that's an impossible task!"

"We're not paying for the sacred disposal of my Aunt Mabel's barn," said Jynn. "Every hundredth bucket will be checked by our wizard here."

"Will it?" said Pagnell.

"You tell us how much weight of human ashes are in that bucket and we'll pay for the next ninety-nine buckets accordingly."

"That's outrageous," said the priest. "We won't comply."

"Oh, okay," said Jynn. "If only there weren't a dozen other temples in the city offering exactly the same service as you. I wonder if any of them would be willing to take over your contract with us..."

Maegor made to deliberately look at Chrindle. "I see the final member of the council is here, so we should be about our official business."

The priest, realising he was being dismissed, and with little chance of appealing his case, gathered his miserable bucket of grey porridge and slunk out.

As the council took their seats, Jynn wrinkled his nose at Chrindle.

"Are those the same boots you were wearing yesterday?" he said.

"They've been cleaned," she said.

"Oh," he said. "Are you sure?"

Chrindle sniffed surreptitiously. She couldn't smell anything. That either meant Jynn was mistaken or she had become so used the stink of the Turge filth that she'd become nose-blind to it.

"The rebuilding of the city," said Maegor and unrolled a long map that had been much pored over and annotated in recent days. Chrindle was a soldier and was used to reading maps that were changed and redrawn with each engagement in a war campaign. This map was a history of the battle between the city that was, the city it wanted to be, and the grim reality of the current situation.

"Rebuilding has already begun along the Street of the Sisters," said Jynn.

"And our edicts about non-flammable materials and appropriate fire breaks between buildings are being followed?" said Maegor.

"They are," said Jynn. "Though the price of bricks is subsequently going through the roof."

"Why?" said Chrindle. "Have they become more expensive to produce?"

"Hardly," said Cunnan. "With all this free charcoal for firing the bricks lying around."

"No, but as demand for fireproof materials increases, so does the price."

"That doesn't make sense," said Chrindle. "If I was a brick-maker and more and more people wanted to buy my bricks, I could probably afford to put my prices down and still make a good living. I don't think the lord treasurer has done his sums properly."

"And I don't think the master of horses knows how the world works."

"People are looking to make a quick profit from the needs of others," said Pagnell.

"It's thievery," said Chrindle.

"It's not thievery if it's honest," said Jynn. "Honest thievery is called entrepreneurial spirit."

"Speaking of which..." said Maegor.

"Honest thievery or entrepreneurial spirit?"

"It depends," said Maegor. "I noticed that the most

expensive bricks being sold are those stamped with sigil of the Temple of the Dragon."

"Is that so?"

"I gather from one of my little spies that the Temple of the Dragon will offer you lower insurance costs if you build your house with their bricks."

Cunnan frowned as he worked his way through the concept. "The people who are acting like gods will accept smaller offerings in exchange for the same level of protection?"

"One of their priests tried to sell me life insurance this morning," said Chrindle.

"How does that work? If you die, do they promise to bring you back?"

"We don't tolerate the undead in Grome," said Maegor reproachfully.

"It doesn't work like that," said Jynn irritably. "None of it works like that. It's a simple business proposition, a way of protecting your belongings and livelihood."

"By giving money to the dragon god or his insurance salesmen?" said Cunnan.

"But the dragon is no god," said Maegor.

"Believe what you will," said Jynn, "but if you live in the DPZ then you'd be a fool to not take out some form of dragon insurance."

"DPZ?" asked Pagnell.

"The Dragon Prone Zone." Jynn stood up and ran his hands over several parts of the city that had been marked out with yellow hatching. "These are the areas most likely to come under dragon attack."

"How do you know?" said Maegor.

"Because these are the bits that have been burned down or demolished."

"Well, just because a dragon has burned them down once..."

"Lightning never strikes the same place twice," said Cunnan.

"Not true," said Pagnell. "I speak from bitter and personal experience."

"Oh?"

"A foolish few days spent in the Spire Mountains. I still get a high-pitched ringing in my ears if storms are on their way."

"Statistically," said Jynn, "if you live outside these zones then there is no evidence that you are in danger of dragon attack. Inside these zones... well, the ashes speak for themselves."

"And I suppose," said Chrindle, getting a feel for how this kind of business worked, "people living inside the DPZ will be required to pay higher dragon insurance."

"Because of the greater risk," agreed Jynn.

"But this will go down if they use your bricks."

"That's ri— If they use the Temple of the Dragon's bricks, yes."

"But you might be willing to charge them even less if they put iron spikes on their roofs?"

"I could discuss that with relevant businessman," said Jynn.

"Perhaps even offered them insurance protection for free

if they were willing to position a giant crossbow on their roof."

"Free insurance?" said Jynn, nearly choking on the words.

"The city gets a free crossbow emplacement. The owners get free insurance."

"And what's in it for me — I mean the insurers?"

"Tax exemptions," offered Pagnell.

Jynn looked at the wizard. "Tax exemptions?"

"And perhaps guild status so that not every Tom, Dickon and Ary can go into the insurance business."

Jynn stroked his stubbly chin thoughtfully. "Yes. Maybe."

"Now, this rebuilding of the city," said Maegor, "allows us to re-plan the main thoroughfares."

"Too many straight lines for my liking," said Jynn.

"Yes, we've already established you like things crooked."

"Gives 'em character."

"Yes, well, all of these old alleys, runs and ginnels will be swept away. We shall have wide boulevards, wide enough for four carts to pass with ease."

"Waste of space, if you ask me."

"Open spaces will act as firebreaks," said Chrindle.

"And give people the ability to move about without knocking elbows all the time," said Cunnan.

"Over-rated," said Jynn.

"We have four new roads running north to south and likewise east to west," said Maegor.

"Killing the natural organic character of the city."

"It is happening, lord treasurer," said Maegor firmly. "The only question we have to answer regarding them is what to call them."

"Do we get to name them?" said Chrindle. "I thought street names just sort of ... happened all by themselves."

"They may develop their own nicknames over time as certain trades move into the area, true. Steel Street's proper name is Lord Jaffleton Way. Similar goes for Silk Street, the Timber Road —"

"Knee-Trembler Alley," said Jynn.

"That is its actual name," said Maegor. "Garmond 'Knee-Trembler' was a much feared general to King Rogar."

"Oh," said Jynn, surprised. "I assumed otherwise."

"Nominative determinism," said Pagnell.

"What's that?" said Jynn.

"If your street name's going to give you free advertising, it might pay to set up shop there."

"But these new roads," said Maegor, trying to steer the debate back round.

"Slap some kings' and queens' names on them," said Cunnan.

"Name one after our new king or queen," said Chrindle. "Once they've decided which of them it will be."

"Are kings and queens that popular at the moment?" said Pagnell.

"Dragon Street?" said Cunnan, running his finger through the most heavily damaged section of the city.

"Might bring back painful memories."

"Perfectly Safe from Dragons Street," suggested Chrindle. "That'll reassure them."

"That's not how human minds work though," said Cunnan.

"Brad Bowman Boulevard," said Pagnell.

They considered this.

"In recognition of the city's saviour," said Pagnell. "And a reminder of the importance of a well-prepared and well-armed citizenry."

"That is good," said Jynn.

"It sends a positive message," agreed Maegor.

"They're singing that song in every tavern of the city," said Cunnan. "People are starting to embellish the legend with their own accounts."

"Very good."

"Although Lady Forge has a new song that's doing the rounds. *How the Wizard Singed his Sausage.*"

"Really?" said Pagnell. "She wrote a song about my experiments."

"Aye, well," said Cunnan and laughed. "You think it's about a wizard with a sausage but really..." He hooted with laughter. "Really, it's not about a sausage at all!" He broke down in breathless laughter and slapped his knee.

Jynn smirked. Maegor frowned contemptuously. Chrindle had no idea what the man was laughing about.

"If it wasn't about Pagnell's sausage..."

"It's not about *my* sausage," said Pagnell.

"It's clearly a reference to your sausage."

"My sausage is not a fit subject for song."

"Cos this wizard's sausage..." panted Cunnan and then could say no more, gripped by uncontrolled mirth.

"My sausage is of no interest to anyone," said Pagnell firmly.

"I'm sorry to hear that, mate," grinned Jynn.

"Filthy, filthy..." said Maegor.

"I don't get it," said Chrindle.

"He puts it..." wheezed Cunnan. "He puts his sausage..." But he could barely breathe now.

"Please, gentlemen," said Maegor. "The streets! The streets!"

"First, second, third, fourth street," said Jynn, perhaps tiring of the debate.

"That's just showing lack of imagination," said Maegor.

"Maybe," said Pagnell loudly, trying to avoid looking at the red-faced Cunnan as he finally calmed down. "Maybe we should name them, as many cities do, for the nearest town or city you'd reach if you travelled in that direction." He looked at the map and thought. "Carius Street, Yelzen Street."

"Yelzen's a thousand miles away," said Chrindle. "You would pass through many towns before you reached it."

"But Yelzen is the one everyone's heard of."

"Red Salka downstairs might disagree with you there. If she becomes queen and discovers you don't think Castle Grimvale is worth naming a road after then there'll be trouble."

"Fine. Give them all a road. Every petty squabbling thane you've got."

"But who gets the best road?" said Cunnan.

"Maybe they could pay to sponsor a road of their choice," said Jynn, his eyes lighting up at the prospect.

Maegor not only shook his head at that but his whole body, setting his chains rattling.

"We'll have none of that nonsense."

"Then no names," said Pagnell. "North Road, South Road, East Road, East-South-East Road."

"Well, that would make sense," said Maegor.

"Quite a lot of sense," said Chrindle. "If you're walking along North Road then you're going north."

"Unless you're going the other way," said Jynn.

"But then if you're going south down North Road, you're heading towards the South Tower, so you know you're going south."

Pagnell's brow was furrowed. He pawed the map. "That's the North Tower of the castle surely," he said, pointing to the tower of the northern corner of the castle."

"No, that's the South Tower," said Chrindle.

"What? The most northerly tower of the castle is called the South Tower."

"Yes," said Jynn.

"Aye," said Cunnan. "It's obvious."

"Obvious?" said the wizard.

"Naturally," said Maegor. "If one is stood in any of the main market squares of Grome and you want to know which way is south then you look for that tower."

"South Tower," said Jynn.

Pagnell stared agog. "I've been looking in the wrong place!" he said, got up and ran out.

The privy council watched him go.

"And they say wizards are clever," said Jynn, tutting.

13

"The South Tower!" Pagnell hissed to himself as he ran to the northern end of the castle. "The South Tower! Stupid bloody Gromish!"

He found the tower. It too had not gone unscathed in the dragon queen's assault on the city but the stairs were whole and he bounded up them at speed.

"Dragon roost, dragon roost," he sang to himself under his breath.

As with the tower at the southern end of the castle — he wondered if it was called the North Tower — there were many rooms on the floors of the South Tower at the northern end of the castle. He popped his head in rooms, scanned for dragon signs and ran on. If he definitely had the right tower then he felt the dragon's nest would be in a most obvious place.

As he ran, his toes stumbled on the stairs. Fat ridges of stone ran along and down the steps. He put his fingers to them. They were cold and smooth, like a fat worm that had been petrified in the act of slithering downstairs. He pressed on. The weird worm ridge was joined by another and a third and then, as Pagnell inspected the steps again, he realised they were warm.

Melted stone.

The dragon had blasted this tower with fire several days ago, sending rivulets of molten stone running down the stairs. Only now was it cooling. He trod more carefully.

The top levels of the tower steamed. His feet were warmed through his boots. When he bent to touch the floor it was uncomfortably hot.

Around the final bend and the wall had been melted away completely, stone solidified once more but with the appearance of a dried mudflow, of day-old custard. From here, Pagnell could see the entire city, the walls and the plains of the kingdom beyond. Winter was coming and the fields were bare. Pagnell was not afraid of heights but he had a very healthy respect for them. He cleaved as close as possible to the inner wall of the spiral staircase without actually burning himself against it. There would be no point in coming up to this eyrie only for a rogue blast of wind to send him toppling off the side.

The top of the tower was a blasted ruin. The floor a concave hollow melted by dragon fire. It hissed in the rain. There was a small mound of rubble at its centre. Pagnell would have crawled over but that would have set fire to his knees. His feet were starting to complain at the heat already.

He whipped off his coat and his jerkin. He tied one around his left foot and the other about his right and moved in a pathetically timid crouched shuffle to the centre of the exposed roof. The rubble was hot. Fearing he might run out of clothing soon, he slipped off his over-shirt, bundled it arounds his hand and carefully prised stones away.

The dragon egg was a perfect ovoid, as big as a prize-winning marrow and the striking yet delicate blue of a clear spring morning.

"Oh," breathed Pagnell, "the teeth we're going to clean with you!" And then he giggled because even wizards are not beyond the occasional giggle.

He laid out his over-shirt, rolled the egg into it and tied it securely before lifting it up and beginning the long journey down. Once he was safely at a spot where there were actual walls, he stopped to take the jerkin and coat off his feet. The floor was still hot but there was more danger of him tripping over his bound feet than burning himself. As he leaned on a window ledge for support, he looked out and saw a commotion in the courtyard below. Crowds had gathered. There were flags and banners. And was that the sound of bugles and drums rising up on the wind?

"We'll be glad to be out of this place, won't we?" he said to his egg and continued down the stairs to investigate.

14

Newport Pagnell entered the throne room at pretty much the same moment as the privy council and the leading edge of the band of cityfolk, who had all but stormed their way inside. The thanes, who had spent the past handful of days alternating between feasting and arguing, drinking and debating, groggily sat up and tried to look like the nobles they were supposed to be.

"What's going on here?" demanded Maegor.

"We have come to proclaim the new king," said a small nasally man in golden priestly robes.

"The new king will be proclaimed when he — or she! — king *or queen* will be proclaimed when the thanes of Grome have determined which of them should take the throne."

The thanes tried to nod sagely at this but were generally ignored by the crowd who booed Maegor's words.

"It is we who have come to proclaim the king," said the priest.

"Any proclamations will be given by me," said Maegor stiffly. "As master of seals, it is my duty to make royal —"

"Master of seals?" said the priest. "You mean, like..." He honked and flapped his hands together.

"Not that kind of seal!" snapped Maegor but the crowd were all doing it now.

"Does he train them to balance balls on their noses?" someone shouted.

"He's fat enough to be a seal anyway!" shouted another.

"Not that kind of seal!" Maegor yelled, totally losing his cool and breaking the first rule of how to deal with a hostile crowd.

"If he just called himself master of scrolls or something similar, it would avoid all this confusion," Pagnell whispered to Cunnan.

"There's going to be trouble," said the old sailor turned lord admiral.

Chrindle put her hand on her sword hilt.

"This doesn't have to end in violence," said Pagnell. "Let's see what they want."

Chrindle was about to offer some comment and then saw the bundled dragon egg Pagnell was carrying.

"What the hell is that?"

"Toothpaste ingredients," he said.

"Who would you declare as king then?" Maegor shouted at the crowd. He probably meant it to sound mocking and belittling but the little priest took it as an honest enquiry.

"The saviour of the city!" the priest said.

The crowd cheered.

"The hero of the people!"

Another cheer.

"The one…"

Cheer!

"… the only…"

Cheer!

"… Brad Bowman!"

The crowd clapped and whooped and hollered and parted to let a young man through. He was tall, athletic and handsome with a shock of blond hair that shone like gold. He wore clothes that would have been traditional huntsman garb except they were clean and finely woven and dyed an expensive vibrant green. He had a quiver of arrows over his shoulder and a longbow in his hand. He regarded the thanes and the privy council coolly and then tossed his head to throw his beautiful hair back. If ever there was a hero of the city then this young man certainly looked the part.

Maegor whirled on Pagnell, wild-eyed.

"You said he didn't exist! You made him up!"

"We've all heard the songs," said the priest. "We all know what this young man did for the city."

"*The arrow did fly and struck the dragon true! The beast turned tail and away it flew*!" sang a woman's voice from the midst of the crowd. Pagnell knew that voice. Everyone in the city knew the voice of Lady Forge.

"And some of us we were lucky enough to see him in action," said the priest.

"You?" said Cunnan. "You saw him?"

"Not me specifically but my friend, Hotpot, said his brother saw the fateful arrow fired."

"My sister's neighbour's mam saw it all!" shouted a voice from the crowd.

"My uncle two streets over was there and watched Brad wrestle the beast!" shouted another.

"Wrestle it?" said Chrindle.

"My uncle saw it!"

"Aye, and the baker's boy's blind grandma!" shouted another.

"Ain't she blind?"

"But she 'eard it!"

The crowd erupted with competing claims of who had best witnessed the heroics of Brad Bowman.

"What the hell is happening?" Chrindle hissed at Pagnell.

"Our plan worked too bloody well!" said Cunnan. "We promised the city a hero..."

"But he's a figment of the wizard's imagination," said Chrindle and then gasped. "*You* said, you said wizards turned up unexpectedly and..." She gasped again. "He's magicked Brad Bowman out of his head into reality!"

Pagnell, who recognised that shock of blond hair, and knew that a good bath and a clean set of clothes could work wonders, looked around for Jynn and saw the lord treasurer and most enterprising thief in the city, loitering by a balcony, away from the centre of attention. A smile danced at the corner of his mouth, faintly, invisible to any who weren't looking for it.

Pagnell sidled over to him.

"This is your doing," he said.

"Don't know what you're talking about," said Jynn

happily. "Although, it was you who suggested we put a dummy on the throne."

"That's one of the castle staff, not a dummy."

"Oh, I don't know about that. The boy's under strict instructions to keep his mouth shut. Good kings know when to keep their mouth shut."

"It's not the sole requirement!"

"No, but if they've also got sound financial backing and a wise advisor beside them…"

Maegor and the priest were arguing in an undignified manner in the centre of the room. The crowd of city folk were throwing in their jibes and heckles as they saw fit. The thanes were slowly waking to the fact that they might soon have a new king and it wasn't going to be any of them.

Red Salka, thane of the far north, climbed onto a trestle table, kicked aside a dish that happened to be in her way and shouted at the assembled crowd. She was not a large woman, did not have a loud voice but there was something about the young flamed-haired lass with a steely gaze that drew folks' attention.

"People! Gromishmen! This is no way to behave! You cannot march in here and declare that this man is your king!"

"We have!" shouted someone, emboldened by the fact that they were somewhere near the back and couldn't be seen.

"Kings and queens are drawn from the long lines of the noble houses of the land! I have my titles because my father held them before me and his father before him and all the way back to Bon the Builder."

"And how did he get to be a lord, eh?" said the priest. "By taking the lands from the first men who settled the land."

"And we're taking the throne now!" shouted out another invisible voice.

"No, you can't!" said Red Salka. "Because... because that was then and this is now. We're more civilised now. We don't do things like just take someone's land because we're stronger than them!"

"What about the war against the Grey Islands? That was only last year!"

"That's different," she said petulantly. "They're *foreigners* so it's okay."

"You was foreigners too before you invaded this country!"

"Shockingly perspicacious for an unruly mob," Pagnell said to Jynn, impressed.

"If you want a decent mob, you do have to pay for it," said the lord treasurer.

"I really don't think I could allow this to go ahead, all the same," Pagnell said, apologetically. "Puppet kings with a kleptocratic power behind the throne aren't good for a kingdom."

Jynn's smile broaden and Pagnell saw he had his dagger in his hand. Pagnell hadn't even seen him draw it.

"You do use a lot of big words, wizard," said Jynn, "but I don't see how you're going to stop me."

"No, me neither," said Pagnell but then, as the crowd set up a chant of "All hail King Brad! All hail King Brad!" all proceedings were interrupted by a bombastic roar from outside.

Being by the balcony, Pagnell and Jynn were the first to

see but were soon joined by councillors, priests, would-be kings and phony kings and the politically motivated folk of the city. Below them, the solidified Turge River had erupted, the great plug of sewage exploding skywards in a pustulant and powerful fountain.

"By the gods!" exclaimed Jynn.

"Glasswort sudanum actually," said Pagnell. "I did think it would be too powerful."

The explosion had sent clods of excrement, great and small, hurtling hundreds of feet into the air and flying out in all directions.

"Watch out," said Cunnan, drawing back into the cover of the crowd. "Some of it's coming this way."

Pagnell was fortunate enough to be able to step sideways into the shadow of a pillar. Others were less fortunate. Crud rained down on the castle walls. Jynn, who Pagnell recalled saying that having toilet slops thrown into the street kept the populace on their toes, clearly was out of practice. A clump of high velocity poo smacked him in the face, breaking his crooked nose and coating him in crap.

As he staggered about and the crowd behind moaned and wailed at the soiling they'd been subjected to, events continued apace down in the streets. With the plug ruptured, the weight of the Turge headwaters and the lake that had being forming behind the dirty dam, forced their way through, carrying boulder-sized lumps of solid muck before it.

"Is that effluvium on fire?" said Chrindle.

"Ah," said Maegor delighted that he was both untouched

by the shower of dung and able to offer a scholarly view. "Human and animal excretion both produce marsh gases that when exposed to naked flame —"

"He's lit the farts of the whole bloody city," said Jynn miserably, prodding his bleeding nose.

The wave of rolling, flaming filth surged through the city along its old course. People ran from the on-coming tide of stink. Items that had been left on the river banks — carts, stacks of timber, piles of rubble, temporary stalls and tents — were picked up and carried with the mass.

"For a wizard who says he doesn't do bangs and poppers," said Cunnan, "that's quite a sight."

The fireball accelerated, smoke and steam billowing in its wake as the fresh river pursued it through Grome.

"Some of those buildings nearby..." said the dragon priest.

"There may be some collateral damage," Pagnell conceded as the mighty mass of manure swept all before it.

"But the Temple of the Dragon..." said the priest.

"No," said Jynn, pushing muck from his vision. "No, that's not allowed. Please, gods, no..."

"But you've got insurance, haven't you?" said Chrindle.

The wall of fecal force tore along the mud banks, eroding in an instant that which could have stood for another century. The flagstone before the Temple of the Dragon slipped into the froth, the foundations of the building itself giving way a moment later and the gold-plated statue of the dragon —

"Not the dragon!" wailed Jynn.

The statue toppled forward into ordure and flame and the boiling river and was gone without a fight. As the diminishing poo ball of fire moved on towards the harbour, the remains of the Temple of the Dragon, Jynn's gilty side-business crumpled floor by floor, priests jumping for their lives from the windows, the more mercenary-minded clutching money bags as they did. All rolled into the River Turge. Pagnell (as best he could see from this distance) was relieved to note that priests, those unencumbered by gold at least, floated well enough.

Fire fizzled in the deep harbour and then went out.

Stunned silence prevailed on the balcony of the throne room, broken eventually by Brad the Bowman.

"Do I still get paid, Mr Jynn?" he asked.

Jynn made vigorous head-slicing and silencing gestures at Brad but the ruse was over.

Chrindle grabbed 'Brad Bowman' by the elbow. "You're coming with me, sunshine."

"I was only doing what I was told," the boy sniffled.

"And I'm sure the lord treasurer can help us with our enquiries too," said the master of horses darkly.

Jynn found himself suddenly surrounded by a half dozen thanes who had very nearly seen the throne that none of them wanted slip from their grasp. The crowd of Brad supporters, including the nasal priest, were doing their very best to slip away into the shadows.

"Hey," grinned Jynn with determined affability, "I'm sure we can discuss this civilly. I'm sure there's deal to be struck."

He and his proxy king were hustled away by red cloaks.

"I knew that going into the god-faking 'insurance' business would end badly," said Chrindle.

"The gods do move in mysterious ways," said Maegor.

"As do wizards," said Cunnan, winking at Pagnell and tapping the side of his nose.

"Oh," said Pagnell. "No. Nothing to do with me."

"Of course," said the lord admiral with playful sarcasm. "Nothing to do with you. A wizard turning up just at the right moment. A wizard with no bangs or poppers." He chuckled to himself.

"No. Really," said Pagnell.

"That's right, my lord," said Cunnan and gave him yet another exaggerated wink and nose-top.

"He's pretending," said Chrindle to Cunnan. "Being all terribly humble when he's just done some amazing magicks."

"I know," said the lord admiral. "Very wizardy thing that."

Pagnell sighed. There was no convincing some people.

"It appears we owe you some sort of thanks," said Maegor, in the tones of one who wasn't really sure if this was the case but was prepared to go with the flow.

"Thanks. No. Nothing for me, except..."

He juggled the warm egg in his arms and pulled aside the shirt to reveal it to all.

"In the circumstances, it's the least we can do," said Maegor. "Our gift to you."

There was a sharp crack. A jagged line had appeared along the exposed egg shell. Pagnell felt something roll and move inside the egg.

"A horse," said Maegor. "We will also give you a horse. A fast one. Can you ride?"

"Er," said Pagnell.

"A fine time to learn," said the master of seals and with polite haste led him towards the door.

"THE ONLY WIZARD IN TOWN" is available for pre-order now.
$$INSERT BLURB$$

ABOUT THE AUTHOR

Heide and Iain are married, but not to each other.

Heide lives in North Warwickshire with her husband and family. Iain lives in South Birmingham with his wife and family.

Heide and Iain have written more than twenty novels together, and love to hear from readers, so get in touch!

ALSO BY HEIDE GOODY AND IAIN GRANT

The Only Wizard in Town

A city under siege by a barbarian horde...

A band of ruthless mercenaries...

A trap-filled dungeon...

A situation like this calls for the best wizard in town.

What they've got is the ONLY wizard in town: Newport Pagnell, oral hygiene specialist.

More used to soothing fevered gums and extracting rotten teeth, this dental spellcaster has to perform an operation like never before: extracting a fabled treasure from the jaws of certain doom. This time, he might have bitten off more than he can chew...

The Only Wizard in Town

Clovenhoof

Getting fired can ruin a day…

…especially when you were the Prince of Hell.

Will Satan survive in English suburbia?

Corporate life can be a soul draining experience, especially when the industry is Hell, and you're Lucifer. It isn't all torture and brimstone, though, for the Prince of Darkness, he's got an unhappy Board of Directors.

The numbers look bad.

They want him out.

Then came the corporate coup.

Banished to mortal earth as Jeremy Clovenhoof, Lucifer is going through a mid-immortality crisis of biblical proportion. Maybe if he just tries to blend in, it won't be so bad.

He's wrong.

If it isn't the murder, cannibalism, and armed robbery of everyday life in Birmingham, it's the fact that his heavy metal band isn't getting the respect it deserves, that's dampening his mood.

And the archangel Michael constantly snooping on him, doesn't help.

If you enjoy clever writing, then you'll adore this satirical tour de force, because a good laugh can make you have sympathy for the devil.

Get it now.

Clovenhoof

Oddjobs

Unstoppable horrors from beyond are poised to invade and literally create Hell on Earth.

It's the end of the world as we know it, but someone still needs to do the paperwork.

Morag Murray works for the secret government organisation responsible for making sure the apocalypse goes as smoothly and as quietly as possible.

Trouble is, Morag's got a temper problem and, after angering the wrong alien god, she's been sent to another city where she won't cause so much trouble.

But Morag's got her work cut out for her. She has to deal with a man-eating starfish, solve a supernatural murder and, if she's got time, prevent her own inevitable death.

If you like The Laundry Files, The Chronicles of St Mary's or Men in Black, you'll love the Oddjobs series."If Jodi Taylor wrote a Laundry Files novel set it in Birmingham... A hilarious dose of bleak existential despair. With added tentacles! And bureaucracy!" – Charles Stross, author of The Laundry Files series.

Oddjobs

Printed in Great Britain
by Amazon